Baleful Beasts and Eerie Creatures

Introduction by Andre Norton

Illustrated by Rod Ruth

Rand McNally & Company

Chicago / New York / San Francisco

GU

Library of Congress Cataloging in Publication Data

Main entry under title:
  Baleful beasts and eerie creatures.

  CONTENTS: Butler, B. The patchwork monkey.—
—Gessner, L. The Yamadan.—Land, C. Monster blood.
[etc.]
  1. Horror tales, American. [1. Horror stories.
2. Short stories] I. Ruth, Rod.
PZ5.B216   813′.0872   (Fic)   76-20529
ISBN 0-528-82171-7
ISBN 0-528-80211-9 (lib. bdg.)

First printing, 1976

contents

introduction

by ANDRE NORTON

Recently there have been many changes in our ways of thinking about the unknown. In a world which gives serious consideration to the investigation of the existence of the Loch Ness Monster, Bigfoot, and the Abominable Snowman, monsters are no longer just a part of superstition. Things once labeled "magic" are known to be "wild talents" which some of us do actually possess—even if they cannot yet be controlled.

Fear, however, remains perhaps the oldest and strongest emotion known to mankind. And that fact has not changed. It is ever at his back, touching him on the shoulder, ready, lurking about the corner to confront him.

We are fascinated by fear—as long as we can keep it under control, our servant rather than our master. Why do so many of us enjoy reading ghost or terror tales? Because therein fear is chained upon the printed page so we are safe and yet can savor the excitement it raises in us.

Some years ago I attended a writers' conference where

there was a discussion of what made up fear. One writer stated that her idea of a truly horrifying experience would be to walk out of one's door in the morning, only to discover that the rosebush planted to the right, now stood on the left. Distortion of the everyday provoked, in her, fear carried to a fine art.

I must admit that I have a taste for the eerie, therefore I welcomed the lucky chance of being able to read the stories in this collection. Who does not relish a shiver or two?

The impact of any story depends upon two things: the ability of the writer to create believable characters and background, and the reader to be aroused in turn when some emotion of his own is awakened. The collection of "Baleful Beasts" herein presented is still extraordinary enough, in spite of our present preoccupation with such material, to raise more than a chill along the reader's backbone.

Here the "rosebush" theme of the accepted and familiar becoming the menacing is used to splendid effect with careful and delicate plotting and evocation of atmosphere in two tales—Ms. Butler's truly malicious monkey, and Ms. Ritchie's evil in a box brought in an everyday fashion by the delivery man. Personally I shall distrust *all* calico monkeys and unexplained boxes from now on.

Ms. Gessner returns to old legends for inspiration, as does Mr. Land. But the Yamadan of the Amerindian tales is quite different from the creature that the hero in "Monster Blood" sees in action and is able to combat because he *does* know his legends.

"Tigger," "You Are What You Eat," and "To Face A Monster" deal with alien surprises either on this world or another under exploration, in which creatures utterly beyond our knowledge are the menaces. One delights in the unquenchable Tigger, a Terran hero wearing fur instead of a space suit, while the strangers of Ms. Bednarz and Mr. Rathjen are formidable enough to provide those who must deal with them a hard battle.

In "Spell of the Spirit Stones," Ms. Wellman returns to one of the oldest legends—that of the werebeast, human and animal in one. But this tale is set in a background springing from the magic and beliefs of a people unknown to most Americans.

We enjoy being just a little frightened as long, of course, as the ghost and the monster remain only the products of gifted imaginations. This collection will provide stimulation for that part of us. It is shivery and strange, and perhaps not to be taken just before bedtime. But read it by daylight and enjoy it as much as I have done.

The patchwork Monkey

by BEVERLY BUTLER

Molly might not have been so angry if it hadn't been raining, but it seemed like the height of unfairness for her
mother to drag her away from her favorite television pro-
gram and send her out in the rotten weather to fetch Jason
home from his tea party with Mrs. Welles. Just because her
little brother was too dumb to know when it was supper-
time, and Mrs. Welles was too old-fashioned to have a telephone, Molly had to suffer.

"It's not raining that hard," her mother said, handing
her a slicker and a pair of rain boots. "And the fresh air
will be better for you than that witch show. I don't like all
this interest of yours in magic and witchcraft, anyway. The
first thing you know, you'll start believing all that nonsense
is true."

"I could believe Mrs. Welles is a witch," Molly said.
"She's probably fattening Jason up for the kill, like in
'Hansel and Gretel.' Why else would an old lady like that
invite a seven-year-old in for chocolate and cookies?"

"Now that's enough of that talk. Mrs. Welles has had a lot of tragedy in her life, and if Jason reminds her of one of her youngsters who died so long ago, there's no harm in letting him help her relive her memories. I want you to be respectful toward her."

Molly yanked the plastic rain boots over her shoes. "I hardly ever even see her. She never gave me even a stick of stale gum. It's Jason who gets all the favors."

"She is odd," her mother conceded, "but you have to remember that she's very old, too. She probably doesn't realize you'd care about candy and gum and comics at your age. You look pretty grown up for twelve, you know."

That wasn't true, and Molly knew it. She was small for her age and had more than once been mistaken for younger than she was. Anyway, it wasn't the candy and gum and cookies she cared so much about—it was the unfairness. She and Jason were the only children on this road. According to the real estate man, there had been no children in the neighborhood for some twenty years. So it wasn't as if Mrs. Welles had singled Jason out from among dozens to be her pet. Besides, it was Jason who got all the favors from everyone. And Molly was always expected to act her age and not care and go sloshing out in the rain on errands nobody else wanted to do. It wasn't fair.

She ran most of the short distance to Mrs. Welles's house, her head bent against the rain and her fists clenched in her pockets. Jason let her in, acting as if he lived there. "Don't come on the carpet all wet," he told her. "Stay on the mat."

Molly stuck her tongue out at him and raised her eyes in swift innocence as Mrs. Welles appeared from the kitchen. From the top shelf of the bookcase a plump rag figure grinned down on her with a mouth of red yarn. Molly's interest was captured at once. "Is that a doll? Or a monkey? Or what?"

Mrs. Welles turned. "Oh, that's Patches. He started out as an ordinary toy monkey, but he wore out so fast that I finally had to make him a new skin out of pieces from the clothes of all the children who ever played with him."

She lifted the creature from the shelf and brought it to Molly for examination. It really was a monkey made of patches. One paw was red, the other a pink candy stripe, and its tail was a long tube of faded denim. Tufts of brown yarn stood out around a face that looked like it might once have been a white stocking. The eyes above the red grin were round black buttons, and a collar of little brass bells jingled around its neck.

"He's taken care of quite a few children in his time," Mrs. Welles said, smoothing a triangle of blue gingham that formed the monkey's left shoulder. "The children come and the children go, don't they, Patches? That's what keeps us young."

Molly touched a flower-sprigged hind foot. "What a lot of different cloth. I'd sit and look at him all day if I had him." She wasn't sure herself if she were wishing or hinting.

"I wouldn't," Jason said. He slid both hands around the monkey's middle, ignoring the fact that Molly was holding it. "I'd play with him."

"Jason," Molly protested, tightening her grip. She glanced up at Mrs. Welles for confirmation that he had been given no permission to take possession.

"Would you, dear?" Mrs. Welles's blue-veined fingers removed the monkey from both children and held him up at a tantalizing height. She tilted her head to smile into the white stocking face, and the reflected light of a lamp shot sparks of fire from her spectacles. "He'd like you, I'm sure. It would freshen him up a lot to go home with you."

For one delightful moment Molly thought Mrs. Welles was about to give the monkey to her. She put it instead into Jason's hands.

I don't care, Molly told herself fiercely. She said it aloud to Jason when they got outside and Mrs. Welles's door was shut behind them. "I don't care. I saw him first, and she showed him to me first, so he ought to be mine if I want him. But I don't."

"Yes you do." Jason patted the bulge where the monkey was zipped inside his jacket and pranced ahead of her through a puddle. "But you can't have him because she gave him to me. She's *my* friend."

"She's not a friend. She's a witch. A mean, spiteful, two-faced old witch. She hates children, but she needs fresh blood from them every once in a while to keep alive," Molly said, stretching her stride to catch up with him.

"You shut up," Jason yelled at her. "You're a witch."

"No, I'm not, but I can tell one when I see one." Molly was inventing easily now, almost as if she were telling a story she had always known. "And that monkey's not a monkey, either. He's her creature that she sends out to gobble up children for her. Every patch on his body is from the clothes of a child he has gotten rid of for her, starting with her own. Just you wait. Tonight at midnight—"

Jason broke into a run. "You shut up, I said. I'll tell Mama and Daddy what you're saying, and you'll be sorry. You shut up."

Molly ran after him. "You'll be sorry when he bites you."

Jason dashed into their yard and slammed the gate shut before she reached it. "If he bites me, he'll bite you, too. Then you'll really be sorry."

But Molly wasn't sorry. She knew that by the time she got the gate unlatched and could follow him, Jason would be in the house, telling how she had spoiled his monkey for him. So what? That would not unspoil it for him—or for Mrs. Welles. She glanced back up the road to where Mrs. Welles's front windows were staring out into the dark like two unwinking yellow eyes—watching her.

A queer prickle down her spine sent her hurrying indoors. Jason was already eating his supper, and Molly's was waiting on the table. She had forgotten that their parents were going out this evening and that she and Jason were going to be alone for a few hours. "And I want no more talk of witches and evil spells while Daddy and I are gone. Understand?" her mother said, stopping Molly as she was about to sit down. "You'll be scaring yourselves to the point where you don't know what's real and what isn't. Anything can happen after that."

Again Molly felt her skin prickle under her shirt. For a second she almost wished her parents were going out another night, not this one. How could her mother be so certain what was real and what wasn't? Molly had given witches scarcely a thought until she moved here where she passed Mrs. Welles's house every day on the way to and from school, but now they were on her mind all the time. Maybe Mrs. Welles actually was some sort of evil creature sending out vibrations for Molly to pick up.

Molly thought about that while she ate, and decided not to think of it anymore until her parents were home again. It was not that she was scared exactly. She didn't think Jason was very scared, either, the way he danced around the living room in his yellow pajamas, waving the patchwork monkey at her after their parents left, chanting, "Nya, nya, he's mine."

"So take him to bed with you and be quiet," Molly said when he had to pause for breath. "Nobody's going to fight you for him. He's too ugly."

And the monkey truly was ugly. She was surprised she hadn't noticed it before. The red yarn mouth was so long and so thin that it looked as much like a snarl as a smile. And the unblinking button eyes seemed to stare right at you no matter where you were in the room.

"I *will* take him to bed with me," Jason said. "If I go. But I'm not going. Not until you do."

He could be stubborn when he wanted to be. Molly chased him into his bedroom five times before she finally got him to scramble under the covers and stay there. She waited outside his door for a while, ready to catch him if he tried getting up again. When all had been quiet for about ten minutes, she peeked inside. The light from the hall showed him sound asleep, his cheek nestled in the pillow, and the old monkey tucked under his chin.

Molly admitted to herself that he was a cute little boy when he was asleep, and she could understand why an old lady like Mrs. Welles could like giving him things. But that didn't give Mrs. Welles any excuse for taking him over as if he were her own, and it was no excuse for being so unfair.

Molly tiptoed downstairs. She was on the bottom step when Jason yelled. Her anger at him came back in a flood. She spun around on the step and shouted up at him, "You shut your mouth, Jason, and go to sleep this instant."

"He bit me," Jason shouted back. His voice quivered as if he were about to cry. "He bit me. Molly—"

Molly ran upstairs and switched on his bedroom light. "Who bit you? You were having a dream."

"He did. The monkey." Jason, sitting on the edge of the bed, fingered his neck. He opened up the yellow collar of his pajamas to let her see a bright spot of blood on his throat.

"That monkey couldn't bite you. Don't be silly," Molly said. "I made that stuff up. That's not a bite, anyway. It looks more like a scratch."

She picked up the monkey from the pillow. Funny, he was heavier than she had thought. A little bigger, too. She held him by his stiff, overstuffed arms and felt something scratch her thumb. There in the end of each paw, almost hidden in the seam, was a pin bent like a hook. Some child of years ago must have thought monkeys should have claws and provided this one with them.

18

"You probably rolled on him in your sleep and got

stabbed," she said, showing the pins to Jason. "Lie down again and forget about it. You'll live."

"No!" Jason said as she started to return the monkey to its place on the pillow. "I don't want him in bed anymore. Put him on the dresser."

Molly couldn't blame him. Her own heart was thumping faster than was comfortable, although that was mainly because she had sped upstairs in such a hurry. She sat the monkey down hard on the dresser so that the blue denim tail pointed up against the wall. Ugly thing, she thought. There was a faint jingle from the bells around the monkey's neck as if in answer, and for just the flicker of an eyelid the button eyes seemed to reflect the light with a yellow gleam.

"I don't want to stay up here," Jason said. "I want to come down and watch television for a while."

Molly considered this. She would be in trouble if he let it slip tomorrow that she allowed him to stay up late to watch television. Still, if she made him stay up here and he scared himself sick because of her stories, she would be in worse trouble. "Okay," she said.

She left him curled up in their father's armchair in the living room and went into the kitchen to heat some water for instant cocoa. Maybe that would soothe him enough to send him back to bed.

When she returned to the living room, a marshmallow-topped mug in each hand, she stumbled over something in the doorway. "That's a dumb place to leave anything," she said as hot cocoa sloshed over her fingers. "Why'd you bring that thing down, anyway? I thought you didn't like him."

She gave the patchwork monkey a kick into the middle of the room. It landed sitting up, facing her.

Jason huddled himself deeper into the corner of the chair. "I didn't bring him."

"Well, I didn't bring him. So how else did he get here?" A little more cocoa spilled as Molly set the dripping mugs in a pair of glass ashtrays. She drew a long breath and added very firmly, "He certainly didn't come by himself."

Jason stared at her from wide, dark eyes. "I didn't bring him."

Molly stood quite still. The monkey had drooped forward so that its front paws touched the floor between sprawled hind legs. It looked as if it were gathering itself for a clumsy leap. A gust of rain spattered against the windows. The drizzle that had been falling all day was growing into a real storm.

"Maybe he *did* come by himself," Jason whispered.

So that was it. Molly suddenly understood. Jason was trying to get even with her for scaring him. He was out to scare her.

"If you're going to be that silly, I'm shutting him in the hall closet where he can't get out. I'd shut Mrs. Welles in there, too, if she was here."

Molly stalked to the monkey, grabbed it by its arms, and marched into the hall. A pain jabbed her fingers. She knew it was from the imitation claws, but it felt like tiny fangs sinking in. It felt, too, as if the monkey were wriggling in her grip, trying to get free, but that, of course, was only the effect of its heavy body swinging from its captive arms. The thing must be stuffed with lead. She needed both hands to thrust it up on the shelf in the closet.

"There." She slammed the door and heard the latch snap into place.

Then she switched on the hall light and another light inside the living room door and a third one on the other side of the room. Not a shadow was left lurking anywhere. Then she twisted the television dial to a channel that filled the screen with dancers in beautiful gowns. Happy party music lilted from the speaker.

"Drink your cocoa," she told Jason.

"I don't want it." Jason was eyeing her fingers. There were streaks of blood on them. "He bit you, too, didn't he?"

20

Molly put her hand to her mouth. The punctures were beginning to smart. "Scratched, not bit. That's a dumb toy to give anybody. It doesn't have to be alive to kill you."

"But what if it is?" Jason asked.

"Is what?" A flash of lightning beyond the windows dimmed the lights for an instant.

"Is alive." Jason gave a strange giggle. He was rubbing the scratch on his neck again. "What if everything you said is really true?"

"That's crazy. And you're crazy to believe it." Molly wished she had closed the drapes, but she didn't feel, somehow, like walking to the end of the room to do it. "The monkey belonged to Mrs. Welles's own children. She wouldn't give an evil thing to her own children."

"Those weren't her own children. She was their stepmother, and they didn't like each other when she first came to their house," Jason said. "She told me so."

And those children had all died as children. How they had died no one remembered anymore; it had happened such a long time ago. Molly had heard Mrs. Stark, the organist at church, telling her mother the old story just yesterday. One child had died from falling downstairs in a fit, Mrs. Stark thought. But nobody was still living who really knew, except Mrs. Welles, and she seemed to go on from generation to generation, never growing any older or getting any younger. Were the patches on the monkey from those stepchildren's clothes? Their clothes and no others?

"Anyway," Molly said a little too loudly, "the monkey's shut away. He can't—"

A roll of thunder stopped her. It started as a rumble that grew and grew until the house trembled. In the midst of it there was a click in the hall. Molly's neck muscles went stiff. She couldn't turn her head to look. But she didn't have to. She knew that the closet door had jarred open.

"It's true," Jason whispered into the silence that followed the thunder. "True, what you said."

"No!" Molly cried. "Don't believe it. Don't."

But they both heard the thud of something falling—or jumping—to the floor from the closet shelf. They both heard the jingle of brass bells.

Molly shot a glance at the living room door. It was still empty. "Run," she said, and she hurled herself toward the opening just as the lights flickered and went out.

Something bumped into her and knocked her down. "Jason!" she yelled.

"Molly! Molly, help!"

He was behind her somewhere, lost in the dark. There were scuffling noises and a crash. He kept crying to her, but his voice seemed to come from first one direction and then another.

Molly was lost, too. A wall met her reaching hands where the doorway should have been. She turned to the right and stumbled against the armchair. Jason was no longer in it. The chair arm and the cushion were warm with a sticky wetness. In the corner of the chair her fingers slid across a glass ashtray like the ones she had set the cocoa mugs in.

"Jason," she called. "Where are you?"

This time there was no answer, no sound anywhere except the lashing of rain against the window.

A flare of lightning showed her the living room doorway. She ran for it and into the blackness of the hall. The edge of the closet door struck her head full force as though someone had pushed it. She went down in a heap on the floor.

When her spinning wits cleared and she could bear to lift her aching head, all the lights were on again. A woman on television was talking cheerily about toilet bowl cleaners. Neither Jason nor the patchwork monkey were anywhere to be seen.

"Jason?" she tried waveringly.

"Up here. In my room." The voice was muffled a bit, but it was Jason's sure enough, and he wasn't crying.

He came out of his bedroom fully dressed as Molly gained the top of the stairs. His eyes were round and black in a very white face, but he was smiling.

"Where are your pajamas?" she asked.

He ducked his head, avoiding her eyes as he tucked his shirt inside his faded blue denim jeans. "I changed them. They got—messed up."

His rumpled hair stood up like tufts of brown yarn. The shirt he had on was the patchwork one their grandmother had given him for his birthday. Molly hadn't ever noticed before that one of the patches was a triangle of blue gingham on the left shoulder. Or that at the throat there was a square of yellow the exact same shade as Jason's pajamas.

"What happened to you? How did you get up here?" She was groping behind her for the stair rail, but she couldn't find it.

"Don't you know?" Jason stretched out a hand still half-covered in a pink candy-striped cuff. "Come on. I'll show you."

"No." Molly raised her arm to ward him off. "Stay there. Stop it. Stop fooling."

He started toward her, his smile growing wider and thinner until it was a red line of yarn across his flat face. He laughed in a silly falsetto that wasn't Jason's laugh at all. "I'm not fooling," the monkey said.

Molly shrank away from the blazing yellow of his eyes. The bells around his neck jingled as he moved closer. "No," she cried once more. "I don't believe you. You're not real."

And she stepped backward off the stairstep—into space. . . .

The Yamadan

by LYNNE GESSNER

The digital clock on the nightstand showed exactly mid-night when Steve Glimson sat up in bed, wondering what had wakened him. He couldn't remember hearing a noise. He didn't have a stomachache. And nobody had turned on a light. Yet here he was, sitting bolt upright in a pitch-dark room—waiting. For what?

Though the summer night air was balmy, he shivered. As though sleepwalking, he slid from the upper bunk and dropped silently to the floor. Beyond the open window only blackness met his gaze. Yet he knew something was out there.

"Phew!" he gasped, clapping his hand over his nose and mouth as he caught a whiff of a musty odor—like rotten garbage.

At the sound of his low exclamation, two lights flickered in the darkness just outside his window. He felt his skin crawl as he stared, convinced somehow that these two glowing lights were eyes staring at him. Yet how could they be? He had seen many wild animals in the woods surrounding the farm, but always their eyes reflected light, they never generated the light themselves. But on this moonless night there was no light to be reflected, and the house was in total darkness.

"What's up, Steve?" came a sleepy voice from the lower bunk.

"Nothing," he managed to say without a quiver. When he slammed shut the window, the two points of light disappeared. Only then did he turn to face his younger brother, Irwin. "Just closing the window because of the stink."

"What stink?" Irwin mumbled. "I don't smell anything."

"You couldn't smell cow dung if you fell in it."

"Sorry," Irwin said into his pillow, and immediately Steve regretted snapping at his brother. It wasn't fun having stopped-up sinuses like Irwin did, and the kid was sensitive about his allergy.

Steve climbed back into bed, but sleep was a long time coming. He kept seeing those two glowing lights. Finally he fell into restless sleep.

The sound of Irwin opening the window woke him, and he struggled off the bunk bed, feeling strangely tired. He looked at the eight-year-old boy, five years younger than himself. Maybe it was because Irwin was small for his age, or because he was a slow learner—not really mentally retarded, Steve insisted to himself, but slow in grasping new ideas. Anyway, it always made Steve feel protective about his brother—a protectiveness he didn't feel for his eight-year-old cousin, Emmy, who was spending the summer with them, or for Adele, his fifteen-year-old sister. He only felt that way about Irwin. But then, everyone in the family had a special feeling for Irwin.

26   The two boys raced to see who would be the first one

dressed, and Steve deliberately put his shirt on inside out, so he had to take it off and put it on again. Irwin's gleeful "I won!" made Steve feel better after the way he had spoken last night.

Steve went with Irwin out to the chicken house to gather the eggs, Irwin's before-breakfast job. On their way back to the house, Steve stopped in mid-stride, staring at several huge footprints in the dirt outside his window. His dark hair felt stiff at the roots, and his body was suddenly clammy. Automatically he wiped his hands on his jeans. Through his mind flashed thoughts of the terrible creature the local Indians called the Yamadan, the monster that lived in the forest. He glanced around, expecting to see the burning eyes, but all he saw were Adele's two horses rounding the house at full gallop. Adele was on one, Emmy was on the other.

Dodging, he leaped up on the back porch step and yanked Irwin up with him, yelling at his sister for being so reckless. Irwin found the momentary excitement amusing, but Steve's thoughts were still on the footprints. They had been obliterated.

"Are you okay?" Mom asked when Steve came into the kitchen. "You look pale." She touched her hand to his forehead, but felt no fever.

"You'd be pale if you had two dumb girls galloping their horses right at you," he snapped. "They could've run over Irwin."

Mom clucked, as she usually did when her children bickered, but she didn't seem concerned.

When they were all gathered around the breakfast table, Steve looked at his square-faced father. "Dad," he began, feeling a little uncertain. His father wasn't one to put up with ghost stories and such. "Have there been any bears around here lately?" Those footprints probably had a very logical explanation.

27

"Bears?" Dad said, looking up while he nibbled a strip of bacon. "No—not in the last few years."

"You sure?"

"Sure as I am that hens lay eggs. Not a farm around here has seen a bear—or even a bear print for that matter, since . . ." He paused to think, ". . . since the rangers moved the last of them to the national parks. That's been seven or eight years at least."

Steve's heart seemed to stop for a moment. No bears. His logical explanation dissolved.

"W-what about a Yamadan? They—"

Dad slammed a fist on the table so hard that the dishes clattered, and Irwin timidly shrank in his chair. Automatically, without being fully aware that he was doing it, Steve put a hand over Irwin's. His younger brother smiled and resumed his silent eating.

"Yamadan! Yamadan!" Dad growled. "A lot of Indian gobbledygook. Horned beasts that walk like man, mysterious disappearances, moss-draped forest—utter nonsense!" He glared at Steve. "Look for yourself. Do you see moss hanging from the trees in our woods?"

Steve shook his head. All of the surrounding woodland was filled with oaks, birches, and other more delicate trees. Yet Indian legends said that these very woods, the home of the Yamadan, were dark, dank, and draped in ghostly moss.

"What brought this subject up?" Adele asked in the imperious tone she had been using lately.

"Steve's trying to scare us because we scared him," Emmy suggested, and she grinned tauntingly, showing a mouthful of braces. Steve ignored her.

"I'll have no more talk about the Yamadans," Dad said sternly, nodding toward Irwin who was busy eating his oatmeal. Then in a gentle voice he added, "I won't have him frightened. Do you understand?" Steve nodded and concentrated on his breakfast.

When the meal was over, Steve went out to do his chores. Theirs was known as a truck farm, growing mostly corn, melons, and squashes. And back toward the woods was open pasture land for their cows.

"When you finish your chores around the house," Dad said, "I could sure use some help. How about harvesting the ripe corn?"

Steve nodded as an idea formed in his mind. When he finally got to the cornfield, he hurriedly filled his big bags with the ripened ears, and then left them, darting off beyond the pumpkin patch to the clump of trees where old Nobara lived in his log cabin. Nobara claimed he was an Indian chief, but there wasn't much left to be chief over. Only six Indians, the remnants of what was once a proud tribe, still lived in this grove, and Dad didn't like Steve to hang around them. He said they made up stories that frightened the neighboring children, and that it was only at the sheriff's insistence, that they kept quiet. But today Steve needed information.

The old chief sat on the stoop of his cabin by the front door. Though Nobara wore the conventional jeans and plaid shirt of his neighbors, he still preferred moccasins to shoes, and he tied a red silk band around his gray hair. His dark face was all lines as he smiled a welcome, but his eyes held the usual deep sadness. Steve had often wondered what tragic event in the old man's life had brought such grief to him. As far as he knew, Nobara had never fought in any wars, nor had any of his immediate family been massacred. Yet he must have known some great sorrow.

Today, as usual, the old man seemed pleased to see Steve, and he talked of the little squirrels he was trying to lure closer to eat the acorns he had gathered for them.

"Nobara," Steve said when there was a moment of silence, "does the Yamadan make huge footprints . . . sorta like a bear?" He tried to steady his voice.

"Big tracks," Nobara said, nodding, "but two—not four like the bear."

"What kind of . . ." Steve hesitated, shivering despite the heat. He wanted to know, yet he was afraid to find out. "What are its eyes like?"

For a moment Nobara looked startled. "Eyes? Why do you ask about its eyes?"

Steve shrugged. "Oh, I don't know," he said carelessly. "I just wondered, I guess. I've heard that the Yamadan is big and hairy, and that it has horns, and claws for hands. But I never heard about its eyes, and eyes are important. You can tell a lot by eyes."

"Like fire," Nobara said in a low voice. "Eyes like fire."

"Have you ever seen a Yamadan?" Steve asked, remembering the red glowing lights of last night.

The old Indian shook his head. "If I had, I would not be here to talk with you now. To see it is to die. In all time, only one man ever saw it and lived. That is why I know how it looks."

"Who saw it?" Steve's voice cracked.

Nobara, looking uneasy, shuffled his moccasined feet. "My father's brother."

Steve's eyes widened in surprise. "Tell me about it," he pleaded.

For a long time Nobara said nothing. When he finally spoke, his voice shook with dread. "The Yamadans—there are two, both males—they are necessary to each other. When one dies, the other must get a new companion."

"How?" Steve murmured, feeling goose bumps.

"It steals a man . . . or a boy. It changes him into a Yamadan."

"It stole your uncle?" Steve asked in awe.

Nobara nodded. "When I was only a boy, my uncle

disappeared. He came back a few days later and told about

the Yamadan—said it lives in a wet, gloomy forest with much moss. He said he began to change—to grow horns and hair on his body—and he begged the Yamadan to let him go home. Uncle talked to animals. The Yamadan understood and let him go."

"Do you really believe that?" Steve asked, terrified, but remembering his father's scorn.

"Before my uncle disappeared, he told us he saw the Yamadan's footprints, and eyes like fire." A shiver ran through the old man. "Then he disappeared."

Nobara looked up. His face was suddenly closed. "I will tell you no more. The sheriff-man says I should not talk. But I know the Yamadan lives in the woods. I know. I know."

Though Steve pleaded, Nobara refused to say any more. So he returned to the field and dragged his bags of corn to the wagon Dad had left nearby.

After a quick lunch, Steve was so busy helping Dad that he had little time to think about legendary creatures. Maybe it was the influence of his very practical, hard-working father, but as the day wore on, Steve began to feel that both the footprints and the lights must have logical explanations, even though he might not know what they were.

That afternoon, after the work was finished, he and Adele rode the two horses out to the pasture to round up the cows. "Let's take a quick ride along the edge of the woods," Adele suggested with a mischievous grin.

"Race you," Steve challenged, and off they went, heading toward the beautiful, flower-decked woods. In and out among the scattered trees and shrubs they dashed, yelling and cheering their horses on.

Suddenly Steve's horse skidded to an abrupt stop, almost unseating him. Then it reared on its hind legs, pawing the air and screeching in terror. It reared and danced, backing away as though afraid to pass an invisible barrier. When Steve tried to heel it forward, it suddenly bucked, and Steve went sailing over its head.

"Steve!" came Adele's wail. That was the last he heard as his body seemed to crash through a solid wall.

When Steve opened his eyes, he stared in bewilderment, wondering where he was. Catching a whiff of the rotten garbage smell, he sat up. The surrounding gloomy forest was almost choked with underbrush and junglelike growth. Long whiskers of gray-green moss hung like shrouds from the trees.

Turning to find the source of the smell, Steve stifled a scream. Out of the shadows came a big, hairy creature with goatlike horns projecting out of a melon-shaped head. Beneath eyes like live coals were a flat nose and a big slit of a mouth.

"The Yamadan!" Steve leaped to his feet and turned to run, but something knocked him down. He glanced back but the Yamadan had not moved. Once more Steve tried to run, but again he toppled backward, feeling as though he had slammed headlong into a brick wall.

A wall—a barrier—something the horse wouldn't cross but that he had crashed through. Instead of panic, his father's sensible calmness settled over him. He tried to figure out what had happened. Had he somehow been thrown through an unseen barrier? Where was this jungle? Only one explanation—not one Dad would arrive at—came to mind. Somehow he had crossed a time barrier. He had no idea what time period he was in, but it certainly contained a strange creature.

More curious than afraid, Steve glanced back at the Yamadan. It was ugly with its big round head, its blazing eyes, its clawed hands, and its immense feet, but it didn't seem vicious—at least not at the moment.

When Steve looked at his own body, he breathed a sigh

of relief. It was normal. "Well, what happens now?" he said.

The Yamadan responded with a wheeze. The creature turned and slowly walked away, looking back, beckoning Steve. Curious, Steve followed, scrambling, tumbling, and climbing over the tangled logs and underbrush. Because he couldn't travel fast, they didn't go far, and to Steve the heat and humidity were oppressive.

He heard a commotion, and as if he were up on a mountain, he watched Dad, Mom, and Adele ride up to the edge of the woods, hunting for him. Adele was almost hysterical, insisting that Steve had fallen unconscious at this very spot.

"But now he's gone," she cried.

"Maybe he's gotten up and gone home," Mom said, and she rode back to see. In a short while she returned, sobbing. "No—he's not there."

"Well, he's got to be *somewhere*," Dad said. "People don't evaporate." Steve called out, but even as he did, he knew they would not hear him. Reluctantly they rode away.

When the forest began to get dark, Steve gathered some branches and made himself a bed. Then he lay down, aware of those glowing eyes watching him. He was hungry, but he hadn't found any food. The Yamadan, it seemed, ate only vegetation. But Steve didn't think he was hungry enough to eat leaves.

Trying to fall asleep was difficult. Steve thought of his family. Poor Mom had been terribly upset, and Adele blamed herself for suggesting the race. But Irwin—Irwin was the one who worried Steve most. The boy would be alone in his bedroom tonight, and he didn't like to be alone. Maybe Dad would sleep in the upper bunk, Steve thought, though Adele would be better. Irwin felt safer around Adele. He loved Dad, but his father sometimes scared him. Not that Dad ever yelled at Irwin. He never even raised his

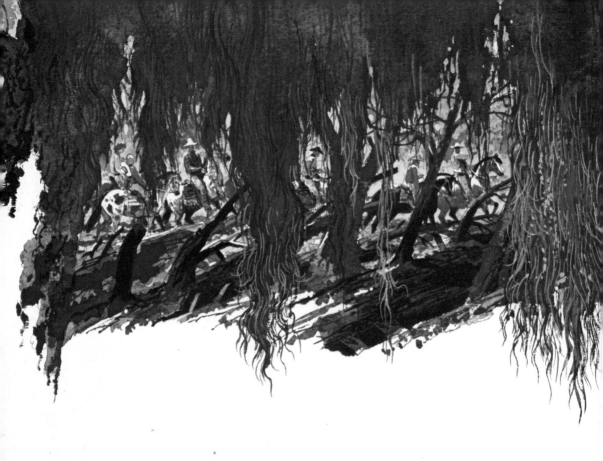

voice. But he yelled at the rest of them and that bothered the timid little boy.

When daylight crept weakly through the dense overhead growth, Steve got up, ravenously hungry. In a small clearing he saw a huckleberry bush loaded with plump, dark berries. Reaching out to pick them, he paused with his hand in midair.

"Oh no!" he squawked, his blood seeming to freeze. His arm was hairy! He tore open his shirt, horrified to see long brown hair covering him. Savagely he grabbed at it, feeling pain as he pulled the hair. But it did no good. Shivers shook his body, and he clutched the shirt front over his hairy chest, hoping that by hiding it, it would go away. He moaned in anguish.

But hunger was stronger than dismay, and Steve

stuffed the berries into his mouth until there wasn't a single one left. Only then did he look for the Yamadan who was squatting by a small swampy pool drinking the brackish water.

All day Steve followed the hairy monster. Twice he saw Dad and some troopers off at a distance, searching the woods. But he was too far away to hear their words. And the next morning when he tasted some leaves, he had to admit that they didn't taste bad at all. To his horror, though, his hands were becoming clawed.

"No, I don't want to be a Yamadan!" he screeched at the monster. "I want to be a boy. I want to go home. Dad needs me to help out."

But the Yamadan merely wheezed and plodded around. And Steve, though he couldn't wheeze back, was beginning to understand.

"I don't want to understand you," he cried out, but it was useless. He was afraid that by the time he could communicate to the Yamadan that he wanted to go home, it would be too late. By then he would *be* a Yamadan, and most likely he would be satisfied with his fate. He probably wouldn't even remember that he had ever been a boy—or had even known Dad, Mom, Adele, or Emmy. Would he even forget Irwin?

Steve wondered how Nobara's uncle had made himself understood. "He talked to animals," Nobara had said. So Steve talked and talked. But it did no good. By nightfall he was growing horns, and his head was getting big and round.

The next morning Steve ate leaves and enjoyed them. He even played games with the Yamadan, and he enjoyed that, too. Scrambling over the undergrowth was not so difficult now, and he didn't notice the steamy air.

"I don't want to be changed," he pleaded. But the Yamadan only wheezed noisily, and Steve understood it to mean, "We're going to be good friends."

Just then Steve heard a voice call his name. He raced to a spot where he could see people moving below. He saw Dad with Irwin, Adele, Mom, Emmy, and several of the sheriff's men. But it was Irwin he watched. It was Irwin calling him. In anguish he realized he could no longer understand the words his brother was saying, but the boy's voice was plaintive.

Steve turned to the Yamadan, his heart aching with longing to comfort his little brother. "You've got to let me go," he pleaded. "Irwin needs me—more than you do. Don't you understand? I'm needed at home." He felt his own eyes burning . . . glowing. . . .

The Yamadan seemed to be thinking back to the companion he had just lost and how much they had needed each other. "You can go back," his wheezing seemed to say. "I'll find someone else. Here, I'll take you down to them."

Then the Yamadan picked him up, and even as they traveled, Steve realized that his own body was slowly changing back to normal. He tried not to breathe as he was clutched close to the stinking body, but the stench invaded his nostrils anyway. Suddenly the Yamadan lifted him high and tossed him forcibly away. Crashing into something, Steve blacked out.

When he came to, he was in a sunny glade. He staggered to his feet, aware of voices in the distance, and he began to run toward them through the sun-dappled woods. In a short while he saw his family.

"Dad—Mom!" he yelled as they rushed to him.

"Are you all right?" Adele demanded.

"You poor dear, you must be starved." Mom was tearful and hugged him close.

"You must've had a concussion," Dad suggested.

Everyone talked at once, firing questions at him. Irwin wound his arms around Steve's waist and stared up at him rapturously. "You'll come home now, Stevie?" he begged.

"You bet," Steve assured him. "I'll be in the top bunk tonight."

"Where have you been, young fellow?" a trooper asked.

Without thinking, Steve blurted, "I've been with a Yamadan in the jungle." But after one look at Dad's shocked face and a reassuring glance at the sunny woods around him, he grinned sheepishly. "I don't know where I've been. I guess I stumbled around and got lost. I've had some weird dreams."

Yes, he decided, that's what really happened. He had talked to Nobara and had his head filled with all those crazy, scary legends. After being knocked out, he had come to while Adele had gone for help. Then he had wandered off and gotten lost, imagining himself turning into a Yamadan.

No one had a better explanation, so by the time the troopers had gone, and the family had settled down, Steve was convinced that the whole incredible incident was the result of his being knocked out in the fall.

That night he lay in his upper bunk, listening to Irwin's quiet breathing. Adele had told him that in his absence she had slept in the room, hoping to calm Irwin enough so he would sleep. But it hadn't worked—he had cried all night. Now, with Irwin at peace, Steve was content. In moments he fell into the first sound sleep he'd had in days.

The next morning Steve overslept. When he woke up, he realized Irwin was gone. Dressing quickly, he went to the kitchen and made himself breakfast. No one was around so he went out to the barn.

"Where is everybody?" he asked Mom.

"Your dad and Adele are out harvesting corn. Emmy's driving the cows to pasture," she replied, gathering the eggs.

"Where's Irwin?"

"I haven't seen him. I thought he was still asleep."

Steve opened his mouth, then snapped it shut. No sense in alarming Mom. Maybe Irwin was in Adele's room.

He raced back toward the house, then came to an abrupt halt. Footprints—big ones—in the dusty yard! All the horror of his days in the dark forest rushed in on him, and involuntarily he tore open his shirt. His chest wasn't hairy! And his hands were normal. But he couldn't control the shivers that ran over him. It *was* the Yamadan! One really *did* exist! But why was it here? Fearfully he glanced over his shoulder, but there was no big hairy creature there. In a state of panic he dashed beyond the barn and looked out across the pasture. There was Irwin riding the horses with Emmy, driving the cows before them.

He grinned in relief. Boy, he was letting this Yamadan thing get to him. A few big footprints and he had almost gone bananas. Irwin must have gotten up after Mom left the kitchen, then joined Emmy when he saw her going out to the pasture. Their laughter drifted back to him.

Steve started out to the cornfield to help Dad and Adele, but they were at the far end. He saw Nobara sitting on the front step of his cabin, and on an impulse, Steve hurried over.

"Tell me more about the Yamadan," he said, feeling foolish, yet wanting to hear the story.

Nobara looked frightened. "No, I dare not. I'm forbidden to speak of it."

"You said it had horns. Were they like antlers?" Steve persisted.

"No—like goats."

"And a head like a melon?"

Nobara gasped. "You have seen it?"

"And it stinks like garbage?"

The old man seemed about to faint. "Yes—like garbage." His bony fingers clutched Steve's arm. "You saw the Yamadan?" Then he shook his head and closed his eyes without releasing Steve. "No—only one man has ever seen it and returned."

"I saw it."

The ancient eyes snapped open. "You saw the Yamadan," he repeated in disbelief.

39

"At first I became covered with hair, then my hands became claws." Steve went on, "I began eating leaves—"

"Yes, yes, the same as my uncle." The old man stiffened. "If he let you go, who will be the new Yamadan?"

"He said he'd find someone else." Steve wondered at the old man's obvious fright. "When your uncle returned, who took his place as the new Yamadan?"

There was a long silence, and suddenly Steve realized that the expression in the old man's eyes was not just sadness. There was a sort of horror.

From the depths of Nobara's frail body came the whisper of a voice. "My father. The day my uncle returned, my father saw footprints and the eyes of fire. He told me. I never saw him again."

Steve felt his legs turn to rubber. Dad! Would Dad be turned into a horrible hairy monster? Dad, who didn't believe in such things?

Steve went racing to the cornfield where he saw Adele. She was alone. "Where's Dad?" he croaked in fear.

"Heading over to the pasture. He's worried about Irwin."

"Irwin? Why?"

"Just before Dad and I started over here, Irwin came out of the house and told Dad he had seen funny eyes last night. Dad's afraid Irwin is coming down with a fever or something."

Steve felt as cold as marble. Before he could organize his tangled, horrified thoughts, he heard Emmy's scream cutting across the farm.

"Irwin's hurt. His horse threw him—in the woods! He's out—cold!"

"No!" Steve cried out in agony. "No, Yamadan, not Irwin! Not Irwin!"

With glassy eyes he watched Dad race to the woods. It was too late.

monster Blood

by CHARLES LAND

Monsters were something you believed in or you didn't. Keith Volmer was a believer. He was a monster buff. Some guys collect bugs or stamps, but Keith collected monsters. And he didn't settle for just any monster like Frankenstein or Wolfman. Keith devoted himself to the basilisk—the horrendous monster of the Middle Ages.

Once Keith began to specialize on the basilisk, he soon learned to know and value the works of Professor Zembeck, world authority on the subject. And as he xeroxed illustrations or diagrams from the Zembeck tomes, the professor took on heroic proportions in Keith's mind. So when he read that Professor Zembeck had actually rented Abbot Castle as a retreat to house his books, ancient manuscripts, and artifacts, Keith was determined to meet him.

Riding his bicycle up to the castle gate, Keith stared at the stone tower, brooding and silent in the afternoon shadows. Though he knew his plan was way out, he was determined to go through with it.

The wrought-iron gate sagged open. Keith chained his bike to a rusted iron scroll and walked resolutely to the massive oak door. In T-shirt and jeans, he looked like any boy out to find an after-school job.

He pounded the bronze knocker, shaped like the head of a hideous gargoyle. The hollow sound was enough to summon the dead. He pounded again and again until, at last, a small window in the door opened. Two eyes drilled through him.

"What do you want?"

"Do you need any help, sir?"

"Go away, boy." The tiny window snapped shut.

Suddenly it opened again. "How old are you?"

"Twelve, last July."

The huge oak door swung back. "Come in! I'm Professor Zembeck."

In the great mirror across the hall, Keith saw the professor look him over. "You're a well set-up boy," he said. "I can use you."

Keith felt the magnetic power of the man. Although not much taller than Keith, he seemed to bend over him. His domed forehead and long stringy hair added height to his slender body, and his voice boomed with authority.

"Tell me, boy, what is a basilisk?"

"It's a monster, half rooster and half snake."

"Very good," the professor murmured. "Basilisks are little known today. How are you so knowledgeable?"

"I collect monsters. Pictures that is. I am a Zembeck fan. I have xeroxes of every monster picture of yours I can find. Maybe you'll autograph one for me."

The professor looked pleased. "Well, well, I think I can even do better than that. But we have work to do. Let's get on with it."

Keith followed Professor Zembeck across the flagstone floor to the tower arch. The tower smelled musty and damp.

It wasn't as old as it seemed. Fifty years ago the ancient stone farmhouse had been remodeled into a castle by a family who wanted one. Now it was hard to rent. People didn't live like that anymore.

"I have some fragile material to unpack. Are you a careful handler? What is your name, boy?"

"Keith Volmer."

"Keith will do well enough. A good Scottish name. My godfather's name was Keith."

The professor seemed to run out of breath as they climbed the spiral stone stairway. Keith was full of questions, but he thought it best to keep cool and listen. At the top of the stairs, Professor Zembeck pushed through the red velour draperies.

"Come in, boy." Keith wondered if the professor had already forgotten his name. "Come in, come in," the professor repeated, and Keith followed him into the tower room. Boxes were everywhere. An ornately carved chest stood in the center of the room. A long worktable was pushed against the wall. Beside it stood a refrigerator. It was then, looking beyond all this, that Keith saw the cage— large and strong enough for a gorilla.

Professor Zembeck's eyes seemed to give Keith a careful appraisal. Picking up a carton from the floor and handing it to Keith he said, "Open it."

Keith put it on the table gingerly. "Is it a basilisk?"

"It's a Jenny Haniver—a fake basilisk," explained the professor. "During the sixteenth century there was a ready market for basilisks. Malefactors created monsters out of skate and ray fish. By adding a few feathers and a snake, these creatures could be made to look like basilisks—or what folks *thought* basilisks looked like. Open it up and take a look."

Keith carefully peeled off the gummed tape and opened the carton. In a sealed specimen case, under glass, lay the most loathsome creature he had ever seen.

"Yuk . . . I'm glad it's a fake."

"You will note," the professor said, "that the face of the ray has a vaguely human appearance. By pulling and snipping—and adding feathers, a length of snake, and a rooster's head—we come up with a pretty good basilisk."

"So that's a Jenny Haniver," Keith said.

"I have the most extensive collection in the world. In these boxes are bits and pieces of creatures to be put together. Most are not mounted. You will find it fascinating work."

Somehow, Keith's plan was not working out. He had come to see a monster, not to cut and paste a collection of fakes. His glance rested on the steel cage.

"What's that for, sir?"

"Ach, I almost forgot. That is for the chest. Give me a hand. We will push it into the cage."

The chest was a masterwork of intricate carving. As Keith's hand gripped the oak surface, the carved snake squirmed under his palm. The thing was alive. The chest became a writhing mass of serpentine horror, but the professor didn't seem to notice. They pushed the chest up to the cage.

"Now we lift," the professor said.

As they set the chest down in the center of the cage, Keith saw a carved rooster's head on the top of the lid. The beak was open, but completely sealed with wax. There was a brass inscription beneath it.

Keith asked the professor what it said.

"Read it. Ach, I forgot boys are not taught Latin nowadays. What a pity. But it's just as well. We have work to do."

"But Professor Zembeck, I *have* to know."

"Why?"

"The wood snake on the chest came alive in my hand."

The professor's eyes radiated excitement. "Ah, this is most interesting. Then you indeed are the one to know. Any boy can handle the unpacking, but you have sensitivity—you are the one I have been looking for. It is your *destiny* to be here."

Keith became more and more uneasy. Standing in a cage with this strange little man was almost frightening. "Professor, how could anyone know what a basilisk looks like? If you see one you're dead. Even a basilisk can't look at himself in a mirror, or he's dead."

"Bright boy. My reasoning exactly. That's why I collect Jenny Hanivers. My search led me to this—"

"The chest?"

"It's not really a chest. It is the carved coffin of the only basilisk in existence."

"Wow!" Keith said. "Is it alive?"

"No, but that's why I hired you. You will help make it come alive."

Wondering how this could be, Keith followed the little man to his workbench. The professor seemed to be searching for something.

"How did you find the chest, Professor Zembeck?"

"My studies led me to a manuscript written by a scholar in the sixteenth century. In it was an account of the carved coffin and its basilisk. It took me years to trace it down."

"But who could capture a basilisk without looking at it?"

"A blind man," said the professor. "A blind wood-carver carved the coffin. Then, with the help of a wizard, he enticed the basilisk into it."

In the lower cabinet the professor found what he was looking for. He pulled out a pair of dark glasses.

"A real wizard?" asked Keith.

"All scientists were called wizards in those days, especially if they worked in the dark arts. This unknown wizard wrote the inscription on the coffin."

"You said you would tell me what it says," Keith reminded him.

The professor polished the dark glasses. "Very well. Translated from the Latin it reads: 'From the cock's mouth remove the wax. Then pour in twelve ounces of cock's blood, mixed with one ounce of youth's blood. The youth must be twelve years and his blood freely given.'"

Keith felt his heart pumping like crazy. "What happens then?"

"The monster will break out of his wooden cocoon and we will cage a basilisk."

"Yeah, but we'll be dead."

The professor waved the dark glasses. "Not so. These lenses have magic qualities. Made in ancient China of ink crystals, they ward off the evil eye."

"Even of a monster?"

"What eye is more evil than a basilisk's?"

Keith bit his lower lip and looked straight at the professor. Even though he knew the answer, he had to ask the next question. "Ah . . . where are you going to get that blood?"

The professor flashed Keith a knowing smile. "That is not a problem." He went to the refrigerator and took out a glass rooster half-filled with blood. "I have ready the rooster's blood. *You* have ready the youth's blood." He laid down the spectacles and picked up a glass beaker. "Won't you give an ounce for science? With your blood, a basilisk will come alive."

"Is that cage strong enough to hold him?" Keith asked.

"Steel was not yet invented when the basilisk lived. It will hold him. This will be the scientific discovery of the age. We will have the living wonder of the ancient world." The professor's voice was lilting and persuasive. "It's a great moment in life to be twelve years old. This is when a boy sees into his own manhood and has a clear view of what is before him. Can't you see the two of us in Stockholm sharing the Nobel Prize?''

Keith had set out to see a monster, and now fought against his fear. If the price of a ticket was his own blood, he was willing to pay for it. "Okay," he said, "I'll do it for science."

Keith helped set up the camp cot and stretched himself out on it. Professor Zembeck expertly drew the ounce of blood from his arm, and though Keith had no feeling of weakness, the professor told him to lie quiet while he put away the cotton, the rubber hose, and the syringe. That bright red liquid in the glass beaker was *his* blood, and he watched as the professor added it to the blood in the glass rooster. Seeing his own blood mix with the blood of a fowl, Keith felt strange.

The professor smiled down at him. "At midnight this mix of blood will bring a basilisk back into the world. We will be famous."

A shiver went through Keith. He got up from the cot.

"Take these," said the professor. He handed Keith the evil-eye glasses. "You will need them to work around the basilisk. I had two pairs put into modern frames—the ancient tie-on temples were hard to manage. Oh, and here is a case for them. Now you can put them into your pants pocket," he said.

Keith felt bewildered. "Thanks a lot."

"You'll make a fine assistant. Come, I'll let you out." Keith followed the professor down the stone stairway. Through the slit window of the tower he could see a flash of orange sky above the trees.

Professor Zembeck touched the switch by the door. The entry hall was flooded in light. He took out a ring of keys and removed one. "Let yourself in when you come tomorrow after school. I can't hear this knocker from the tower room." His domed forehead shone in the light.

"Yes sir."

"Goodnight. I'll see you tomorrow."

Keith rode out of the grove of trees onto Circle Drive. Some cars already had their lights on. He was late for dinner.

His parents were at the table when he rushed into the family room. "I've got a job," he announced proudly.

His father looked up, pleased. "Really? Where?"

"Out at Abbot Castle."

His father put down his fork. "Not for Professor Zembeck?"

"Yes. I'm to help him unpack some stuff."

"What stuff?"

"Jenny Hanivers. He has cartons full of them."

"What are they, dear?" his mother asked.

"Fake monsters. Fishermen used to make and sell them as curios."

His mother looked concerned. "Has anyone ever pointed out to you, Keith, that in the Dark Ages monsters were really the manifestation of evil?"

"No one ever saw one—I guess."

"That doesn't mean they were not used to influence the minds of men," Mrs. Volmer said.

Keith was annoyed but curious. "How?" he asked.

"By the evil eye. Superstitions about it were encouraged, and some people used it to manipulate others. Thank goodness the evil eye is not one of our modern problems."

Keith could tell that his father, too, was disturbed. "Look," he said, chewing his food thoughtfully, "I'm glad you have what it takes to go out and get yourself a job, but tomorrow I'll drop by and have a talk with the professor."

"Why?" Keith demanded.

"Oh there's some gossip about. Some say he's not right in the head. I'll talk to him and let you know."

"He's okay," Keith said. "I talked to him."

"That will make two of us." His father's voice was firm.

Keith was behind schedule with his homework. He kept thinking what his father had said about the professor. Of course people would think Zembeck a nut. Folks didn't believe in old-fashioned monsters anymore. Instead, they have new ones like the Abominable Snowman, or the Loch Ness Monster, or flying saucers. But at midnight there would be another monster around, and it would come to life with *his* blood.

Keith also couldn't stop thinking of the evil eye. His mother's remarks worried him. Surely he would be protected by the Chinese glasses, but would he also be responsible for the monster's return? Would he be accountable for his blood—for what the basilisk might do?

He shivered. The evil eye would be back in the world again—the monster serpent of evil. He thought about it with mounting concern. It would have his blood, with his consent. No prize was worth it. He must go and beg the professor not to bring the monster to life. The basilisk had long been forgotten. It must remain that way.

At ten o'clock Keith shut off the light in his room and climbed into bed with his clothes on. He waited in the dark for what seemed like hours. When the luminous hand on his bedside clock pointed to eleven, he heard his door being pushed open. He snorted a snore through his lips, and minutes later, the light in his parents' room blacked out.

For what seemed an eternity, Keith lay waiting. When he could stand it no longer, he slipped down the hall to the back porch and opened the inner door to the garage. He rolled his bike back through the porch and out to the cement walk. Rubber tires and sneakers made no noise. Keeping to the side of the road, without lights, he became a silent shadow, spinning under the trees. That was his undoing.

Keith had stayed on Circle Drive because it was lined

with trees and he would be unnoticed by passing cars. But he overlooked parked cars. Almost running into one, a battery of lights hit him in the face.

"Where do you think you're going?" The voice was tough, authoritative, and a little amused.

Keith stared into the light, blinded.

"Speak up, boy," said the voice, and when the lights shut off, a police officer stood facing him.

"I'm going home . . . eventually." That last word was spoken under his breath.

"I'll have to write you a ticket," the officer said, "for riding without lights. What's your name?"

"Keith Volmer."

"Address?"

"Twenty-two forty Circle Drive."

"It's pretty late for kids to be out. What were you doing?"

"I have a job."

"You better get on home. Hear?"

"Yes sir." Keith was on his bike and down the road before he had to answer more questions. Luckily, Circle Drive passed the castle before it passed his own house— Circle Drive circled the town.

Keith rode his bicycle up to the castle gate. With only a thin slice of moon in the sky, the castle looked bleak. There was a glow of light behind the draperies in the tower. Was he too late? Quietly Keith laid his bike in the tall grass and started for the door.

Keith fished for the key in his pocket, and the small modern lock opened silently. Keith switched on the lights. Carefully he put on the evil-eye glasses, and with the utmost caution, entered the stairway.

Climbing the steps one stone at a time, Keith felt his way along the wall. What had happened? Everything was quiet as a tomb. When his eyes became accustomed to the dark, he climbed faster and faster.

Reaching the red draperies, Keith carefully parted them. At that moment an alarm clock on the workbench began to ring. A cry stuck in Keith's throat as the professor poured the blood from the glass rooster into the cock's mouth.

Like splintered glass, the wooden coffin exploded. The professor leaped through the door of the cage, but the basilisk was upon him. Frantically, he tried to close the cage door, but the monster slammed it back against the bars with its powerful wings, flattening the professor like a steak on a grill.

Keith tore the draperies apart and let out a whoop. The basilisk turned its feathered head. The baleful eyes and monstrous beak made Keith yell even louder. The uproar worked. Dropping the professor, the monster started for Keith.

Down the stairs Keith fled. He could hear the scratching claws on the stone steps and he could smell the sickening smell of the basilisk as it advanced. His heart pounded, and the smell made him weak and sick to his stomach. His mouth was dry and bitter. He could barely swallow. How close was the thing behind him?

Keith plunged into the entry hall. The blazing lights seemed undimmed by his dark glasses. He backed against the huge mirror, his eyes focusing upon the stone staircase. In hypnotic fear Keith waited for the monster.

The tail of the basilisk—writhing and hissing between its feathered legs—came first, followed by the malignant cock's head, more horrible than the counterpart rattlers on the tail of a rattlesnake. Then out of the shadows came the body of the winged reptile—a gory horror of yellow feathers. Cold terror froze Keith against the mirror.

The monster's eyes, shining with greenish luster, turned on Keith, while the smell—the nauseous stench—permeated

the entry hall. With its horrible head thrust forward, the creature came closer and closer. Lifting its limpid eyes to the mirror, the basilisk saw its own face. Instantly it exploded into an eruption of yellow feathers. The hissing sizzled into silence while a pool of monster blood formed at Keith's feet.

Keith was aroused out of his shock by a man's voice. It was a policeman—the same officer who had given him the ticket. His parents were close behind. The three stared at him. They stared at the feathers and the blood.

"Are you okay, son?" his father asked. "The officer phoned us about you and your bike, and we guessed you'd be here."

Somehow Keith found his voice. "Professor Zembeck needs help." Steadying himself, Keith started for the tower room. Followed by the others, he felt drawn up into a whirlpool of evil. At the top of the stairs, the red velour draperies framed a view of the giant cage. The door of steel bars was shut tight. Wild-eyed, Professor Zembeck cowered in the corner of the cage. He waved his arms.

"Don't open the door!" he shouted. "An unholy monster of evil is loose in the world. He will come back for me. He has broken my glasses. The evil eye will destroy me!"

Keith took off his own Chinese glasses and handed them through the bars to the professor. This quieted him.

The officer snapped the lock on the cage door and put the key in his pocket. "It's a sad case. A brilliant man, they tell me." He turned toward the stairs. "Let's get going. I'll send out for an ambulance."

Mr. and Mrs. Volmer each took Keith by the arm as they slowly descended the stone steps. The officer waited in the entry, studying the mound of feathers.

"What's this mess all about?" he asked.

Keith stared down into the yellow feathers and the pool of monster blood. "Just a crazy experiment," he said.

Tigger

by A. M. LIGHTNER

They call me Tigger. I'm a cat. Not one of those little household cats that are sometimes taken aboard a spaceship for the companionship they give. My ancestors were earthside wildcats—often called bobcats—which is why I have such a short tail. But the rest of me is bigger than most space cats and I have a handsome ruff. I'm also a smart cat and have learned to use the bio-thought-recorder. And that is why I've been asked to report on some of my most interesting adventures.

I joined the space service when the call went out for cats. It was recognized that when exploring a new world with unknown dangers, the special senses of a cat—an animal that can see better, hear better, and smell better than humans—could be used to great advantage. Oh, a human can spot a huge monster coming at him. And the many instruments they have can tell if the atmosphere is poisonous or if an avalanche is about to fall. But for the many little dangers—the snakelike animal in the grass, the deadly creature hanging from a bush—there is nothing like the keen senses of a feline. Especially if it's a smart one like me with all the instincts of my wild ancestors.

I've always worked with the crew of the *Condor*, and of all the humans aboard that ship, my favorite is Ellie. That's short for Eloise, but everyone calls her Ellie. Ellie has the loveliest smell. I'd know it from thousands of others on a dark night. Like me, she's only been on this ship a short time. You see, we're both quite young and just starting in this work.

Ellie's crazy about plants. At least it seems crazy to me. She doesn't care where she goes to find a new plant, and she's always on the lookout for plants that can stop bleeding or cure some disease or are good to eat. And when she gets on the track of something like that, she forgets about everything else. Believe me, she needs me to keep her from walking into a mess of angry alien ants or just to help her find her way back to the spaceship.

I go out with some of the other crew members, too, but I like Ellie best. She pays attention. She gives me credit. The others often act as though I don't know anything . . . till we get into a really hot spot, that is. And then they're apt to level everything around with their blasters, and I'm lucky if I can get out of the way.

Ellie, on the other hand, never takes a weapon with her. She says that *we're* the intruders, and if there's any danger she can always count on me to warn her. And anyway, with all her scientific gear, she has enough to carry.

But I've talked sufficiently about myself. If I say any more, they'll cut it out of the report. I know. They think I'm stuck on myself. Well, maybe after you hear this story, you'll agree I've got reason.

This last place we went, something happened that really had me scared. We were in a big dense forest—what the captain calls a rain forest and what Ellie says is the best place to find interesting plants. The trees and the bushes were so thick that after we had gone only a few steps, we were all shut in. Ellie said it was easy to get lost and made little cuts on the trees to blaze her trail. But I never get lost. I always know which way the spaceship is. It's something the captain calls instinct.

Moving slowly through the forest, Ellie was having a wonderful time collecting leaves from every tree and bush, and digging up low plants or pieces of root for her collection. The biggest trees went straight up so high you could hardly see where the branches began, and they had rough purple bark, and blue leaves instead of green.

But there were smaller trees, too, and leaves from these were the ones she collected. Sometimes she climbed them— she's a good climber on the smaller trees. And sometimes I would climb up and go out on a branch to bend it over far enough for her to grab hold and pick the leaves. But busy as I was helping Ellie, I also had to keep a sharp nose and eye out to be sure she didn't get hold of some strange poisonous creature. For mixed up with all the trees and bushes were hairy vines, mosses, and other strange growing things.

After working like this all morning, I naturally began to get hungry. So when Ellie decided it was time for lunch, I was glad. In the deep forest you can't see the sun, and the light is always dim so it's hard to know what time it is. But Ellie had a watch, and she wouldn't let us stop for lunch till it was really noon.

That's another thing I like about Ellie. She's always willing to share. When I go out with any of the others, they say, "You'll get yours when we get back to the ship. One meal is enough for a fat cat like you."

I don't know why they think I'm fat. Ellie says I'm just the right size for a big bobcat. She says the others are critical because they remember the little house cats they grew up with.

This time, Ellie had a fish sandwich and she gave me some of the fish. Why humans like to surround delicious fish with something like bread, I can't understand. But I guess it was best that way because while Ellie had the bread to eat, I had a lot of the fish. Ellie also had some cheese. And she wasn't stingy.

Having polished off every crumb of that savory meal, sitting on a rock I had carefully inspected for stinging bugs, I was busy cleaning myself when Ellie gave a little cough and sucked in her breath. When I looked up to see what had startled her, I found myself face to face with one of those big menaces that explorers like to talk about but usually have never seen. And, though I'm ready to deal with any little menace that may come hopping, crawling, or slithering toward Ellie, I guessed right away that this was way out of my class.

All we could see at first was a face peering out at us through the leaves. It was quite high up, so I could see that the creature was a great deal bigger than I was. And if it wasn't quite as tall as Ellie when she was standing up, its teeth were certainly a lot bigger than hers.

Ellie put her hand out and took a firm hold of my ruff. "Sit still," she whispered. "Maybe it will go away." But I could smell her fear and it made my ruff bristle and the hair along my back stand up. My job was to take care of the little dangers. Now here was a big one, and I began to wish that Ellie had brought a blaster with her. From the way this beast smelled, I knew it wasn't going to go away.

As usual I was right. The leaves slipped aside as the creature came more fully into view. It was big all right— four legs with well-clawed feet, and a body covered with dark blue spots—good camouflage for stalking through blue-leafed forests. It also had a long tail with a purple tuft and sharp claw on the end, and teeth that were certainly not made for eating vegetables. But then something struck me.

The head on the end of a long neck looked like a cat's! In fact the face was not unlike some of my bigger relatives on Earth—lions or tigers. But I had never run into cats before on any planet I had visited. Could this world be different?

Deciding to see if it would understand cat language, I walked toward it, stiff-legged. When I pulled loose from her grasp, Ellie didn't like it. "Come back here, Tigger!" she hissed. "That thing could eat you in one gulp!"

But I kept right on. Since Ellie didn't have a blaster for protection, this was my responsibility. I walked up to the nearest bush and sprayed it liberally with my strongest-smelling liquid. I moved on to the next tree and repeated the action. Monster Cat, as I'd begun to think of the creature, followed me around, sniffing at each place. In doing so, it turned its back on Ellie, and I heard a scuffling noise from her direction. When I looked again, she had shinnied up the nearest tree. Not a very big tree, it was inclined to bend under her. And I noticed with some exasperation that she had left all her equipment on the ground. Such carelessness, I thought. Suppose Monster Cat decided to eat it? What did she think I could do about that?

I turned back to look at the monster and could hardly believe my eyes. It didn't look much bigger than me! What's more, it was rolling on the ground with its feet in the air— an obvious invitation to play. Could I have been mistaken about its size? I had a distinct impression of a *big* creature, but perhaps it had looked tall because it was up in a bush. There was something here I didn't understand. So slowly and carefully, belly close to the ground and nose stretched out ahead, I approached.

Then I heard Ellie calling from the tree. "Tigger! Come back here, Tigger! It's a trap, you idiot!"

I didn't pay any attention. Let her stay up in the tree where she was safe. I was going to get to the bottom of this mystery. Maybe I had been wrong and this was a she-cat.

It was certainly acting like one—a cute little female for me to play with.

Just as my nose was about to touch the stomach of this strange creature, it leaped to its feet, turning completely around as it did so. It stood there facing me, every hair on end and every tooth exposed, breathing in quick gasps. And with every gasp it got bigger . . . and bigger . . . and bigger! Soon it was as big as I remembered it, towering over me. I didn't wait to see how big it could really get. I turned and ran. The monster came after me, pouncing as I would pounce after a rat.

Ellie was yelling at me, "I told you so! I told you! Hurry and get up this tree, you silly, crazy cat!"

Who's crazy? I thought, as I dashed past her and scurried under a bush and around a clump of trees. If I go up your tree with this thing after me, the whole tree will come down. But I didn't try to talk to her. I was too busy keeping a good distance between myself and that horror.

It was then that I began to notice that same strange behavior. The monster was getting smaller! I was able to outrun it as long as it was big and I was small, for I could dive into narrow openings between trees and rocks. But soon it was small enough to follow without any trouble—it was almost down to my size. Everything seemed to shrink except its head and that mouth full of fangs.

I'd never heard of an animal that could change its size like this, but on an unexplored world, anything is possible. This will never do, I thought. It's gaining on me. It's getting through the close cover as fast as I am.

Of course I had another way out. I could really run away and try and find a hole that was too small for it to get into. But that meant leaving Ellie up the tree when I was supposed to be protecting her. And anyway, with all those claws, it seemed obvious that this thing could climb, too. If it lost interest in me, it might climb up after Ellie. And

although I'd had a frightening glimpse of how big this thing could grow, I had no idea how small it could get. With my luck it could probably shrink small enough to follow me into any old hole!

So I just kept moving, running so fast I hardly noticed where I was going. Two big trees loomed up ahead. They were so close together, I just managed to squeeze through. Could the monster follow me? It was down almost to my size now and just made it. A little bigger and it might have been stuck.

That gave me an idea. I began to circle. I could hear it right on my tail and I put on speed. I managed prodigious

leaps from rocks to tree stumps. If I could only make the monster grow big again! I could probably lick it if it stayed small, but I knew it wouldn't—especially in a fight. If only I could make it get big again just as he reached those trees. Fighting would do it. And so might fear!

As I bounced off a rock slide and cleared a small stream, I could almost feel the saliva dripping from that cat's jaws. The two trees were coming up in front again, and suddenly I was inspired. I remembered my bobcat yell. That used to throw a fright into everyone.

I've been trained by Ellie to always lower my voice. She used to tell me about the famous man in the olden days on Earth who said that the bobcat has "a shriek and yell like the devils of hell."

"And we don't want any devils in a spaceship, please," she would say.

But right now, I thought, the devils would come in handy. The trees were close ahead, and just as I reached them and bounded through, I let out my old bobcat scream. I hadn't done it for so long, I thought I might have forgotten. But it came out high and clear, seeming to echo all through the forest in a frenzy of sound.

I heard an answering scream from Ellie in the tree, and when I looked up, I could see her clutching a branch, having almost fallen from her perch.

"Tigger! Tigger!" she yelled. "Are you all right? Did it get you? Come up the tree at once. Oh, why don't you do what I tell you?"

"Because you tell me all wrong!" I cried, looking up at her from the bottom of the tree. "I've trapped the monster. Now come down here fast so we can scram before it gets loose again."

But she couldn't seem to understand what I was saying. I don't know why it is that I can understand humans better than they can understand me. There must be something lacking in their brains. But there it was. And all the while the monster was struggling to escape from the tree trap. It had blown itself up to its biggest size, and while its head was sticking out on the near side of the trees, its body was kicking on the far side, and its long neck was caught firmly in between. It was growling and snapping and snarling, but I couldn't be sure how long it would stay there. Once it calmed down, it would figure out that all it had to do was shrink a few sizes.

62   I was jumping up and down at the foot of Ellie's tree,

trying to get through to her, when I fell over some of her equipment. I stopped and looked it over. What was most valuable to her? Why, the packet of newly collected leaves, of course! Without another thought, I picked them up in my mouth and headed back toward the spaceship.

Ellie yelled after me. "Tigger! Come back! Where are you going with my specimens? Tigger!"

I ignored her, running till I was out of sight. And then I stopped. I heard her scrambling down the tree, but did I hear the monster? Though it was still hissing hideously and seemed to be staying in the same place, I let out another scream, just to be sure.

It was then that Ellie burst through the bushes, carrying the rest of her gear and crying, "Tigger, don't do that! You've already scared the pants off the whole forest!"

I didn't argue with her. She could see where I was, and I lost no time in setting a fast pace back to the ship.

Later that evening, I heard her telling the captain about our adventure. She received a scolding of sorts.

"That'll teach you to go into an alien forest without some kind of weapon!" the captain said.

"Oh, but I do have a weapon with me," she told him. "I have Tigger. He's better than any blaster you take along!"

Yes, that's me—Tigger—the best blaster on the spaceship *Condor!*

The spell of spirit stones

by ALICE WELLMAN

Though we had entered the forest only ten minutes before, the branches of the great trees locked in a dark roof above us, and ropy vines twisted down to block our path. I clung to Jinell's hand as if I were six instead of way past twelve.

Each step drew us deeper into the forest's green mouth. I said, "Let's go back. This wasn't such a good idea—"

"No," Jinell said firmly. "You beg me to go. We go." Her face had set into grim lines, and her eyes held a strange glitter.

She was right about my begging to visit her home village. Dad had driven off that morning, headed for a two-day conference with the other scientists of his group. The American foundation that sponsored Dad's research project in the Pakaraima Highlands of Guyana required quarterly reports on the findings. I waved to Dad until the jeep was out of sight, then I ran to find Jinell.

She was doing the wash behind our camp home.

64   "Come on, Jinell. You can wash tomorrow. This is a great

chance for you to visit your people."

She wiped her perspiring face on her sleeve. "No, Nan-cee. Your father said I should keep both eyes on you while he is gone. We do not go off this place."

"But you promised. You said you must see your brother before the snow lies white on the mountains. And the last time Dad went, you said you'd take me the next time he had to leave."

I knew I was being unfair to remind Jinell of her promises. They had been the when-peace-covers-my-people-we-go-Nan-cee kind. But to the Akawai Indians a promise was a bond, an unbreakable bond.

Jinell sighed. She stuck the wash into the soak water and faced me. "We go now. Dress for rough walking. This is a time for strong steps and eyes wide open."

It didn't take long for me to pull on my thick denim slacks, mosquito boots, and a long-sleeved plaid blouse. I hurried to meet Jinell in front of the house, but stopped short, amazed by the sight of an alien and startling apparition before me—a Jinell I didn't know. Cloth of brilliant stripes hugged her hips, her honey-tan body nude above it, with half-moon breasts nearly hidden by strands of shells and red berries. Bands of glistening green-gold beetle wings wound about her upper arms, and iridescent tree bark dangled from her ears and dark curling hair. She was beautiful.

"I leave my people a shaman, and I return to them a shaman," she said, pointing to the sling of jaguar skin hanging from her shoulder. "We do not go without my spirit powers—my powers as *el tigre*."

The Jinell I knew was pretty but she had always worn the shapeless dresses the Waramadong Mission supplied to their Indian students. The mission served all Amerindian settlements of this part of the Amazon forest highlands, and Jinell had learned English there. She had been with us since

65

we first arrived at the house near the Kamarang River. "Be good to my little girl," Dad had said. "Nancy has no one but me to care for her." And Jinell was good to me, very good.

It was slow going through the forest now. The ground was spongy and a spatter of heavy dew fell on us. "The forest weeps," Jinell said. "It weeps for me."

She walked proudly with long sure steps I had difficulty matching. I'd always hated being small, pale, and blond, and when forest vines caught my long hair, I wished I had tied it up. But I didn't let that slow my pace.

"Jinell, why did you become a shaman if you didn't want to stay with your people?" I looked up at her forbidding face.

Her voice was bitter as she said, "A shaman trains with suffering for two years. One dies before becoming a shaman. I did not leave of my own will."

Her answer left me even more curious about what could have driven her from her people into a routine of house help for Dad and me. A shaman understands the demands and needs of the spirit world, Dad had explained, and through spirit magic protects the people who look to the shaman for leadership. I wasn't surprised that Jinell was a shaman. I'd always sensed an unusual power in her.

Shrill cries burst from the fig tree not far ahead of us. Both my hands gripped Jinell's as I pulled back in alarm.

"Howlers, Nan-cee," she said, and at once a spiteful chorus of the resonant howls of male monkeys and the harsh barks of the females challenged us. I tried to laugh, for the howlers—with all their infernal noise—were quite harmless. But as we walked toward the fig, the screaming gained in volume. Jinell's eyes met those of the dominant male who crouched on a lower limb. His shaggy neck was swollen with the force of his horrible howls.

At once all noise ceased. The silence of the forest seemed unreal, more frightening than the noise. "Why did the monks stop howling?" I asked, moving closer to Jinell.

"I told them to stop."

"How—how did you tell them?" I'd heard no sound from her.

"My total spirit, *Akwalu*, holds power in the forest. It speaks to forest creatures like one to one. Stand quiet, Nan-cee. I give you spirit stones."

I "stood quiet," waiting. Jinell took three stones from her sling of Jaguar skin—two the size of Brazil nuts, the third a tiny red pebble no bigger than a fresh pea. She rubbed the stones between her palms, then blew deeply on them.

"Swallow this." She gave me the red pebble. When I hesitated, she insisted. "Good to swallow. It stay with you all the days you live. Always you can hear the words of my total spirit and always you can speak to me."

The red pebble went down my throat like nothing at all. She put the crystal stone in my hand. "This will free you from bad spirits. And this . . ." The third stone was polished quartz shaded with green. "This . . . think well what I say. This stone will call my forest spirit to help you."

"But Jinell," I protested. "How can I need help from bad spirits when I am with you?"

"What will be will be." She held open the right-hand pocket of my denims. "Put your stones in here. You will feel the rough of the freeing-stone and the smooth of the call-stone. When you face trouble, blow your spirit into the stone and throw it far. My spirit will take it from the air."

We walked on. "We go to my people as I promised you. But Ekjojo, the shaman who leads them now, is the man whose spirits fought my spirits and outwitted them. He made me leave my people. His total spirit holds power in the plains, the mountains, and the water. You and I do not know what he feels against me, but my young brother, grown to full man since I left the Akawai, tells me with his red speak-pebble that Ekjojo's magic grows weak. Time calls me back."

Jinell's voice gained a strange power. "Keep close, Nan-cee. Do not go beyond the touch of my hand. I hold great fear for you."

Light filtered through the trees. We heard the distant sound of laughter. Uncanny and mocking, it grew louder as we reached the forest's end. Though the sunshine splotching the ground was cheerful, the wild unearthly laughter came in sudden peals, and fear rose in my throat.

Jinell must have felt me shrink against her. "The mountain ghouls laugh. Shaman Ekjojo holds a seance. They laugh at his songs. Keep close, Nan-cee. We enter Akawai over the rise."

Quickly we climbed the rise, went down the slope through a stand of heavy bamboo, and came to a clearing within high bushes and palms. Houses of rough bark huddled together—all empty.

Men, women, and children sat motionless around a low platform of saplings. When rustlings rose from a nearby bush, all heads turned to stare. "Ekjojo brings his leaves," Jinell said softly, and she pulled me down beside her in the outer circle.

Almost at once, a robust young man leaped from the bush, strode with an easy grace to the platform, and swept his outstretched hands around the circle of villagers. He was handsome, with thick wavy hair and comely features, yet his smile held lust for power as well as welcome. I could feel it.

He sang, shaking his "leaves" in rhythm to his song. The "leaves"—four large twigs of trees tied together—were like thick pompons of rustling green. He flapped them in a swishing pattern and snapped them in time to his chant.

The dark mottled skins of the great water snake, the anaconda, wound about his red breechcloth. This—except for the many strings of cotton covered with white bird down that dangled over his shoulders and arms—was his only garment.

Jinell reached for my hand and tucked it under her arm. Immediately the shaman's eyes fixed on us and his teeth gritted together in a sinister smile. Hatred flashed from his eyes. He cupped his hands about his mouth and snarled, "swas-i-i-k swoak" into the air above our heads.

I felt as if I'd been struck. Jinell put her hand on my knee and gripped it firmly as a young man with warm brown eyes slid down beside her. He folded his legs in front of him as we had done, and Jinell blew into his ear. I nodded to him, for I knew the muscular youth must be her brother.

Shaman Ekjojo lifted a small barrel. He drank deeply with violent coughing and spitting. From somewhere a whistle sounded. "Shu-ee-ee." The shaman was trembling all over, and the bird-down strings about his shoulders began to crawl like long white worms.

Suddenly wings beat above my head. I looked up to see a giant gray and black bird with a white-down breast hovering above me.

Jinell shrieked. Her hand left my knee and her arms reached out for me.

In that split second when her touch was lost to me, the giant bird swooped. Its beak seized my shoulder and snatched me from her arms. Pumping in ever-quickening strokes, the powerful wings bore me up into cold, dry currents of air.

Jinell's screams followed me, then slowly died away as we headed toward a cone-shaped mountain in the Pakaraima range. My body felt light as the air, and though the curved beak clamped tightly on my shoulder, I felt no pain. Only panic filled me. I could not cry out.

When the mountain loomed close, I could see, above

the tree line, broad sheets of rock with thick plants growing erratically between them. I would be dashed against those rocks any moment now, yet somehow any fate seemed better than this terror.

But no! The taloned feet clutched my waist, and the massive wings thrashed against the chill wind. I hung sideways, barely clearing the rocks, and a hideous chant of croaks and groans over a muffled thudding floated through the frigid air.

The giant hawk carried me over the sharp rock ledge of the mountaintop where I saw a swarm of shapeless nonhuman things bouncing up and down in aimless fashion. Terrible to hear and even more terrible to see, the creatures were as formless as jellyfish, their long tentaclelike arms striking the lava rock of the mountaintop with every bounce. Each thing bobbed to its own time so that the thudding never paused or stopped.

The huge claws of the bird released my waist, its beak opened, and I fell into the center of the ghastly mass. Lying still on the jagged lava, a freezing wind swept over me. I shook with the chill, but the trembling that seized me when I opened my eyes and saw the formless faces clustered above me was worse. Lidless eyes under hairy brows peered at me, and pale straggly beards trailed from the nonhuman blobs. Smacking colorless lips, the creatures made greedy sucking sounds that congealed my blood.

Two bearded things picked me up with stringy tentacles. I felt the sticky mucus on their boneless arms. They lifted me high and threw me to be caught by other gummy arms, and I was tossed on and on like a senseless plaything. Faster and faster they hurled me until I couldn't catch my breath—couldn't scream or struggle. Only pain let me know I was alive.

Each toss brought forth an outburst of the demonic laughter Jinell and I had heard as we came out of the forest.

These, then, were the *wukna,* the mountain spirits. They were once real people, Jinell had told me, but had been ruled by evil forces. Doomed to be ghouls, they wailed for the living to be brought to them so they could suck the blood and drain the human body dry. And they wouldn't stop until it was a shapeless nothing like themselves.

At last the bearded ones tired of their catch-and-toss game. They dropped me on the lava floor, and women things—more terrifying than the bearded men—bent over me. Their mouths opened to show translucent tongues all ridged and beaded like overgrown leeches. They must be the bloodsuckers.

Gasping for breath, I tried to lift myself to my feet. If I could escape the slimy tentacles and run to the ledge of the mountaintop, I would throw myself over. Instant death would be preferable to being sucked dry of life. But the thin mountain air took away my strength, and the freezing blasts of wind numbed me. My arms were like useless rags, my legs without feeling. The hideous women things cackled with delight as I strained to sit up.

Mucus from their jeering mouths dripped on me. Their flaccid arms carried me over the rim of a lava basin toward a patch of murky green water bordered by a frothy scum. Though rumblings in the mountain's heart broke out into thundering booms and the mountain shook, the arms that held me did not loosen their clutch.

Then, like the gush of a newly drilled well, the green water rose in a whirling column. It threw off a stench of rot and death, and my fight for breath became more desperate. I could only manage shallow gasps that did not seem to reach my lungs. Mocking laughter rose up around me.

Then, like an attacking beast, the ghoul who supported my head tore off my shirt. With a groan of pleasure, her ridged, leech mouth fastened onto my left arm. The others waited in turn.

I felt the gentle touch of a hand on my stomach. A faint whisper sounded in my ears. "Jinell," I said, though no word came from my lips. I dug my right hand into the pocket of my denims for the rough stone.

Unbearable cold wrapped about me and my mind went blank. But Jinell's voice came through the oblivion. "Inhale. The stone."

I dragged the stone from my pocket and inhaled. The stone flew from my hand and whistled through the air. Not a moment passed before the swooping claws and strong beak of the giant bird snatched me up—away from the clammy tentacles and the slobbering mouths—carrying me down toward the Akawai settlement and Jinell.

Faster than the wind the enormous hawk flew. As we whizzed over the clearing, I could hear singing and the rhythmic beat of Ekjojo's "leaves," and then the sound of the rushing currents of the Mazaruni River. I felt the waters rise to meet me, and was dropped on the mucky bank. At last, I could breathe.

Dizzy and barely able to see, I crawled away from the spitting water to dry land. The stretch of warm sand between the river and the forest was inviting. I stretched out to rest.

Whether I slept or lost consciousness I do not know, but the touch of a hand on my stomach awakened me. "Nan-cee, Nan-cee, where are you?"

"Here, Jinell. Here on the sand strip by the river. I can't walk." Again my words were uttered without a sound.

"Close by—the cave of the water-papai. The call-stone. Blow."

I dug into my pocket. No stone. Nothing there. Had I lost it during the long flight from the mountaintop? Or had the evil magic of Ekjojo taken it from me? "Lost," I whispered. "Jinell, call-stone is lost."

I turned my head. From the great boulders beyond

me, a shiny green head on a black-mottled neck protruded from a dark opening. It was an anaconda, a giant anaconda. Its iridescent green body—splotched with black—rippled as it slid over the sand. Alerted by my fall, the snake had left its cave to explore. Though the anaconda sees little and hears not at all, its fast-flicking tongue—its organ of smell and feeling—directed it toward the warm meat lying near the river . . . the warm meat that was me.

It was now halfway between the cave and where I lay. I could see its muscle segments grip the sand as it neared. I was paralyzed with terror. The lidless brilliant eyes of the monster fixed on me, and I felt myself sinking under its hypnotic stare.

Then I heard a strange hoarse whisper. "Nan-cee, water-papai draws near to kill. Throw sand in mouth."

No time was left—not a minute—before the gigantic snake would unhinge its jaws. Its saliva would ooze over my long pale hair and seep down to cover me. Its coils would squeeze out my breath, quickly changing me into a rag. I would be easy to swallow.

The terrible head hovered over me. Its mouth, with teeth slanting back to prevent its prey from escaping, opened like a great tunnel. Already a steel-strong coil twisted about my legs and tightened to encircle my hips. With my uninjured hand I scooped up sand and threw it at the flicking tongue.

A threatening roar came to my ears from far away. It was the roar of the Guyana jaguar, larger and heavier than any leopard, the sly ferocious king of the forest.

But threatening roars did not disturb the slow, methodical attack of the monster-snake. Like a shadow, the story of the Guyana boy swallowed by an anaconda just three days before crossed my mind. I, too, would be found within an anaconda, my body deteriorating in its digestive juices. . . .

No sand stirred under the pads of the spotted gold

jaguar as it leaped past my closing eyes. The big cat must have cleared the sandy stretch in a single bound, fastening its teeth on the back of the snake's head.

Almost at once the snake's jaws turned about and its coils released my hips and legs to attack the jaguar. Thrashing and flailing sand, the two huge beasts locked in their fight to the death. And though Jinell had told me that no killer of the wild has the tenacity and agility of the jaguar, *el tigre,* the raging snake tried again and again to coil its tail about it. But the jaguar did not pause for a second—its springing bounds were too quick for the snake's weak eyes to follow. And at last I heard the great cat's fangs tear into the neck bones of the anaconda. A shattering crunch—and the snake became a wriggling massive length beating upon the sand.

As the snake writhed and twisted in its dying struggles, the jaguar bounded away; then Jinell ran from the forest and leaped to my side. Her brown eyes held pity as she knelt and lifted me in her arms. Carrying me to the river's edge, she stooped to wet a cloth in the water. Tenderly she bathed my face and washed back the sand-laden hair from my eyes. Then she plunged my left arm, still oozing blood, deep into the fresh clear water of the river.

"Nan-cee! Open mouth, Nan-cee," she said, and from her jaguar sling she took a coconut shell to drip a cool liquid between my lips.

"Jinell. Oh, Jinell," I sobbed.

"Shush now. You are safe. We go home." As she bore me to the forest path, I saw the monstrous snake body of black and green lying motionless in the sand. "But Dad says the dead snake writhes until the sun sets," I said with wonder.

Jinell slowed her steps so I could look more closely. There, beside the ugly head, were the two pompons of Ekjojo's magic "leaves." "He has gone to join his *wukna,* the mountain ghouls," she said, staring at the snake.

"Where is the jaguar?" I asked. Jinell put her hand on her heart.

"I am the jaguar spirit of the forest." From the sling she took a broad leaf with dark spots. "A *kumala* leaf," she said, holding it so I could see its strange markings. "I chew it to pulp and change into my *Akwalu* spirit—the spirit of *el tigre*."

Never had home looked so good, so wonderfully good to me. After a bowl of stew, and bread hot from the oven, Jinell sponged my exhausted body and put me to bed. *Kumala* leaves made the poultice for my injured left arm.

"Don't tell my father we went to see your people. Please, Jinell," I begged.

She passed her hand over my eyes, and I was lost in sleep. Whether she told Dad or not, I never knew. Dad asked no questions about our two days without him.

Jinell stayed with us only until her sister, also trained at the Waramadong Mission, came to our house to help Dad and me. And though my joy overflowed to know that Jinell again ruled her people as shaman, to bid her good-bye was heartbreaking.

Yet even today I can call, "Jinell, does all go well with you?" And always her red speak-pebble gives me the answer.

"My days pass in peace. My brother soon learns his shaman magic. Our hearts beat sweet songs for you."

The Night Creature

by RICHARD R. SMITH

When I was twelve, I visited my Uncle Ronald in the city as I had done for several years. Coming from a small town, each two-week visit was like a trip into another world—one of giant buildings, huge stores, art galleries, and new people—a series of adventures to be remembered until the following year.

Uncle Ronald was a tall, strong man with unruly brown hair that usually tumbled down over his forehead and a bushy mustache that nearly concealed his upper lip. He was a technician for a large company that developed and manufactured electronic equipment. Although he would have been considered eccentric by many people, Mom and Dad liked him very much and seldom found fault with his ways.

"Call me Ronald from now on," he said as we left the train station. "You're getting too old for that 'uncle' bit. And tonight, after you've rested, I have a special invention to show you."

I unpacked my suitcase, and as we ate dinner Ronald told me about some of the things he had been working on during the past year. We played a game of chess while he drank coffee and I sipped a cup of hot chocolate. The sun settled on the horizon and the city was rapidly growing dark. I could hardly wait until morning when Ronald and I were to visit the new Aquarama.

Ronald won the chess game—but not until after I had given him quite a battle. Feeling drowsy, I said, "What was the invention you wanted to show me?" I couldn't resist yawning, but felt embarrassed because it seemed impolite.

"In the workshop," Ronald said. He led the way to the back room of the apartment and once more I marveled at all the electronic equipment.

During past visits, Ronald had showed me many of his inventions. I had always been interested but had never been able to understand most of them.

"Have a seat." He waved at a chair. I sat and yawned again, feeling completely relaxed. Ronald's eyes were bright with excitement and pride as he said, "Don't be alarmed by what you see. Now . . . watch this." Standing perfectly still, he rose several feet from the floor. Close to the ceiling, he stretched into a prone position and drifted through the air as easily as a feather.

"Levitation," I said.

"Exactly." He smiled and returned to stand beside me.

"Can you levitate other objects?" I asked.

"No. But that may come later."

He placed a helmet over my head and I noticed wires extending to a large machine with gauges. "Touch this lever," Ronald said. "Push it up. Feel the pressure? Nothing will happen . . . the machine is turned off. I just want you to get the feel of it."

The lever was a sliding kind that he had shown me during a previous visit, but this one traveled in a channel beside the numbers one to ten, and I could feel a tension against the lever.

"Would you like to be able to levitate?"

"Yes!"

"When I turn the machine on, push the lever slowly. It's spring-loaded so it'll return to the 'off' position if you release it. You'll feel a tickling sensation. It may hurt. If it hurts too much, take your hand away."

"What does the machine do?"

"It activates a certain portion of the brain. There is no danger. I've tested it thoroughly." He flipped a switch and the machine hummed with power. "Ready?"

"Ready."

"Move the lever as high as you can. Six or seven may be your limit." I moved the lever up. . . .

Two

Three

A tickling sensation in my head.

Four

Five

Electricity . . . almost a pain . . . not quite . . .

"The higher you move the lever, the more effective it will be," said Ronald.

I wanted it to work. Ronald was my only uncle. During the past years he had taken me on trips to places I could never have seen alone. I *wanted* to join him in this new adventure of levitation.

Six

Seven

A flame burning in my skull . . .

Eight

Nine

An inferno . . .

Ten

"Gary!"

Ronald reached for my hand but I released the lever and it slid back to the 'off' position.

"I didn't think you could stand that much." He took the helmet from my head. "Are you all right?"

"Uh-huh." Strangely, I still felt relaxed.

"Can you stand up?"

I rose from the chair.

"Imagine yourself rising from the floor . . . as light as a balloon," Ronald said.

I expected failure on the first try. *But the floor dropped beneath my feet!* I bumped my head on the ceiling.

Ronald laughed. "Very good!"

We experimented an hour or so in the apartment, then he led the way to the roof. Patches of dark clouds scudded across the night sky.

Ronald pointed at the vault of stars and clouds above our heads. "Do you want to try it?"

I knew we could do it—up, up into the sky—as free as birds. . . .

"Hold my hand this first time," said Ronald. "There's nothing to worry about. You aren't afraid, are you?"

"No!"

Feeling a little foolish, I held his hand as we ascended. The roof dropped beneath our feet. I had never been afraid of heights and now, as we rose, I felt an exhiliration I had never known before. Soon we could see the city stretched out far away in every direction, an expanse of shadowy buildings with glittering lights from windows and cars, neon signs, streetlights, and shimmering reflections of the moon.

We rose—up, up, up—through dark clouds into the world beyond. A sea of stars became our ceiling, and the earth far beneath, our floor. We drifted in a faint breeze. I laughed, reacting to the sheer joy of flying. Some distance away, a large jet swooped toward the airport, its lights twinkling, landing beams bursting to life.

"Let's go down," said Ronald. "We can come up again tomorrow night."

We descended slowly and carefully. The clouds scurried not far below, and suddenly we saw the creature. It swirled from a cloud, dark and ominous, immense and powerful, moving toward us. . . .

Ronald drew an object from the sheath on his belt. I had been so engrossed in the novelty of flying that I hadn't noticed his weapon. The creature came closer as if to attack, and Ronald raised his arm, moonlight gleaming on the weapon. A thin blade of bright light suddenly stabbed through the darkness.

The creature vanished in a mass of clouds.

Early the next morning, I awoke to find Ronald sitting by my bed.

"How do you feel?"

"Great!" Last night I had felt exhausted by all the excitement and had tumbled into bed. Now I felt refreshed and filled with a million questions about levitation. "How long have you been doing that?" I asked, sitting up in bed, my heart beating faster as I recalled how good it had felt to float above the city.

"Since shortly after your visit last year. I want to ask you to promise not to tell anyone."

"Why?" I felt disappointed. It would have been terrific news to tell Mom and Dad. They had always been proud of Ronald; this invention would make them prouder. And what a way to show off at school! I could imagine floating higher than the rooftops, the kids staring and squealing in disbelief.

"It's a very extraordinary power," Ronald explained. "Some people can read minds . . . others claim to communicate with the dead . . . and a few can move objects with telekinetic energy. But so far, no one else has demonstrated a power of levitation."

"But . . . why would it be bad to tell people?" I knew that what he said was the truth. I had never heard of anyone levitating himself higher than a building. But I still didn't understand the need for secrecy.

"The world isn't ready for that kind of knowledge," said Ronald. "Some governments might use it for the wrong purpose."

"Oh." Slowly I began to understand how the power could be used by one country against another—not to help mankind but as a weapon in war. "The creature we saw in the clouds . . . what was it?"

"I don't know."

"Have you seen it before?"

"A few times."

"It started toward us. Do you think it would have hurt us?"

Ronald frowned, rubbing his chin thoughtfully. "I'm not sure if it could. Have you ever walked down a street and had a small dog come yapping or barking? Then, abruptly, if you start toward the dog, it runs away?"

I nodded that I understood. There was such a dog on a street not far from where I lived. It came barking at everyone who passed by, and ran whenever someone started toward it. The creature in the clouds had come toward us until Ronald drew the weapon and waved it threateningly.

"What kind of weapon did you use last night?" I asked. "It seemed more than a flashlight."

"I call it a knife-light," Ronald explained. "It focuses a narrow high-intensity beam with a considerable amount of heat. It frightens the creature. I'm not quite sure if it's afraid of the light *or* the heat."

"What kind of creature could it be?" I wondered aloud, remembering the huge, dark form.

"I'm not sure. I've never seen it during the daytime . . . and I've spent hours studying the sky with a telescope. It must hide during the day, appearing only at night."

"Nocturnal," I said, proud that I knew the word. "Like an owl."

"That's right. Owls prey at night. This creature could be similar."

I felt a faint chill and could not help thinking of the thing we had seen as a kind of monster. It had swirled toward us from a cloud as if about to attack. Large, dark, moving quickly, it had seemed incredibly strong and dangerous. In a way I could not quite understand, it had seemed ugly and evil. What did it eat? Birds? Mice? Insects?

"Why hasn't someone else seen it?" I wondered aloud. "If someone had, there would have been an article in the newspaper."

"There may be good reasons for it never having been seen before," Ronald answered, frowning. "If it is nocturnal, as you've guessed, then it would sleep during the daytime. At night it may hide in clouds even when it is active. It would be almost impossible for anyone on the ground to see it. And as for anyone in a plane seeing it—at the speed planes fly . . ."

We looked at each other. Ronald smiled but it was a grim sort of smile. "We may be stumbling upon a creature as rare as the Abominable Snowman in Tibet."

Or even more rare, I thought. This thing had never even been reported. Considering its size and the fact that it lived in the clouds, it was more unique than ghosts, witches, demons, and other supernatural phenomena people have been talking about for centuries.

"Does the creature scare you?" asked Ronald, watching me carefully.

"Uh . . . not exactly." Putting my thoughts into words

was difficult. The thing in the sky was an unknown element. We did not know how dangerous it was. Almost everything in life—traveling in a car, train, or plane—involved danger of one kind or another. Why, a person had to be careful just crossing a street! If you were too cautious in life, you would never go anywhere. I tried to explain, "It, uh, doesn't bother me enough to keep me from flying."

"Good!" Ronald slapped me on the back. "Now, for more ordinary things. . . . What do you want for breakfast?"

"Scrambled eggs. After we eat, can we fly again?" Through the window I could see the morning sunlight, and the idea of flying in the daytime sounded exciting. We'd be able to see for miles!

Ronald laughed. "I'm afraid we can't. Suppose someone saw us? How could we ever explain?"

But we did fly again that night. We did not see the cloud creature and had to return when it began to rain. As we went down the stairs from the roof, one of the elderly tenants, seeing us in our soaking wet clothes, must have thought we were out of our minds.

On the following night, the sky was cloudless and bright with moonlight. "We'll have to be quick," Ronald explained. "We can wait until after midnight and then rise as high as possible before someone sees us. After we've reached a certain height, we won't have to worry. No one will be able to see us after we're a few thousand feet up."

Shortly after midnight, we soared into the moonlit sky. Despite our speed, we heard a shout from the street below. I saw a man and woman pointing. They rapidly became tiny dots, but I could imagine them telling others what they had seen. Ronald said we should land before the news spread. As a precaution, we came down among trees in a park several blocks away and walked back to the apartment.

The weather was so clear that we had to wait several days before we could fly again. During that time, Ronald gave me a knife-light identical to the one he carried. He demonstrated how to snap the sheath on my belt. "We may never need these, but it is best to have some protection," he said.

To avoid the risk of ascending repeatedly from the same place, we took a bus to another section of the city, then rose into the cloud-filled sky. It was a dark night and there was little chance that we would be seen, so we hovered beneath the clouds, drifting with the wind, making minor adjustments in our course as if we were sailboats upon a dark but peaceful sea. The city lay stretched out beneath us, much different in appearance than on previous nights. Now, with the stars and moon almost completely obscured by the seemingly endless layer of clouds, the city resembled a forest of soft black velvet studded with gleaming and glittering jewels.

But the beauty of that voyage ended, for we saw the night creature following—several hundred feet behind and above—lurking under cover of a cloud.

"Take my hand," Ronald said. "Let's see if we can lose it."

He rose higher, into the clouds, and I soon understood why he wanted to hold hands. It would have been easy to become separated in the darkness. I had learned that clouds were much like thick fogs, and though Ronald had said that the power of levitation was permanent and would soon feel as natural as walking, tonight I felt as if we were running.

Occasionally glancing over my shoulder, I could see the night creature on our trail. It came relentlessly in pursuit—dark, ominous tendrils outstretched as if to seize our bodies. I wondered how it had been created—where it had come from. An alien from another world? There were so many reports of UFOs that it might be a visitor from another planet, a strange form of life. A mutation? Everyone talked about the danger of mutations from atomic test

explosions. Was this some sort of monster that had been created by man? Or—was it possible that creatures such as this had existed since the beginning of time, few in number, always hiding, keeping their existence a carefully guarded secret?

I followed Ronald, and though we raced through the clouds, I knew he was not afraid. He wanted only to see if we could outrun our mysterious opponent. Finally we reached the apartment building and descended.

The next night was my last one in the city until next year. In the morning I would be on a train headed for home. I suppose that is why I hated to leave the sky that night, and why, when Ronald said we should return, I held back moments longer, studying the panorama of crystal-clear stars. Above the smog of the city, galaxies were like handfuls of diamond dust sprinkled across the black ocean of outer space.

As I began to descend, I saw Ronald had already

dropped hundreds of feet and was very close to the layer of clouds that hid the city so far beneath our feet. The creature leaped from the darkness as a lion would leap upon its prey. Ronald saw the attack at the last moment and drew his knife-light. I watched in horror as they struggled—Ronald slashing with the thin bright beam and the monster engulfing him with dark tentacles. They fell beyond view.

Drawing my knife-light, I hurried to help, gliding down into the billowy mass that was so much like an impenetrable fog. . . . "Ronald!"

Turning this way and that, I still could not see. The wind whistled in my ears. I had never imagined a wind passing *through* clouds. It drowned my voice and made Ronald's impossible to hear. Blinded and frustrated, turning around and around, struggling to see through this strange murky jungle, I kept sliding until I fell from the mass of cloud, and the city lay sprawled beneath me in its glittering array of neon-speckled shadows.

Ronald appeared nearby and I rushed to his side. "Are you all right?"

"Fine." He sheathed his knife-light. I wanted to ask how the fight with the night creature had gone, but the wind had increased in tempo, whipping around us so we nearly had to shout to be heard. Ronald signaled that he and I should return to the apartment to talk.

As I had a cup of hot chocolate and he drank coffee, my uncle said the fight had been a strange one—much like fighting the wind. "And," he added with a smile, "it isn't anything to be afraid of."

A few months after I returned home, we received the news that Uncle Ronald had died in an explosion at his workshop. I felt sadder than I ever had before. We had been so close—in some ways closer than brothers—and now he was gone. For days I felt lost, hardly able to eat, wanting only to be alone. I could not help but wonder if the night creature had somehow been responsible. And it was strange to know that I was the only human able to levitate . . . that the actual secret of levitation had died with Ronald. It was very lonely.

I flew three or four nights a week, setting an alarm clock and placing it beneath my pillow, awaking, dressing, slipping through the bedroom window, and soaring into the sky at two in the morning while the town slept. As winter came I dressed more warmly and continued my adventures in the star-filled sea. On Christmas Eve I hovered thousands of feet in the air as a fluffy snow fell. My small home town had turned white, spotted with the bright pyramids of outdoor Christmas trees.

The creature attacked when I least expected. Its dark tentacles twisted around my throat and chest. My ears were filled with an eerie shrieking as it became more and more difficult to breathe. My whole body was soon caught in the crushing grip and I struggled to draw the knife-light Ronald had given me—slashing, stabbing with the bright beam. *It isn't anything to be afraid of,* Ronald had said. I swung the beam in a wide circle. . . .

As the suffocating tentacles disappeared, I looked in every direction.

The night creature had vanished.

Real? It had been real. I had felt it, seen it, fought with it. . . .

Still, I wondered. Had I killed the night creature? Or—had it been my imagination? Had a whirlpool of wind tugged at my body while fear itself shaped sight and sensation into an unearthly monster? I was old enough to know that fear could make the unknown seem very real. Was that what Ronald meant when he said the night creature wasn't anything to be afraid of?

Today, years later, I still roam the sky, usually in the early morning hours as the town sleeps. I cannot let a little thing like a fear of the unknown keep me from the vast realm of the sky.

But I always carry my knife-light, and I watch the clouds for a sign of the night creature.

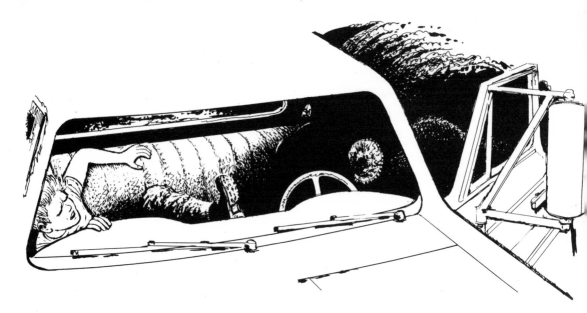

TO FACE A MONSTER

by CARL HENRY RATHJEN

I wasn't enjoying the fishing that afternoon with my Uncle Bob because I knew what was coming. But if I'd *really* known what was in store for me . . .

What I expected was a lecture. The fishing was just to get me relaxed and, Uncle Bob probably hoped, receptive. Of all the people in the McCullum family, Uncle Bob was just about my favorite. But I doubted if even he would understand my problem.

Grandpa McCullum claimed that I, as the runt of the clan, carried a chip on my shoulder because I figured I had to knock down anything bigger than me. In a way he was right. I was constantly in trouble, and even my own brothers and sisters refused to play with me, claiming I was always starting fights.

At school things were no better. My teachers said that though I was capable of getting good grades, I expected too many indulgences because of my size. But as I saw it, they only had time for their "pets." I was not one of them.

In fact, the only person who really tried to understand how it was with me was my Aunt Beth. She is a tiny woman who raises Chinese pugs—toy-sized dogs that look like bulldogs but aren't—and until a few years ago, she and the dogs and I got along real fine.

But on our way to a dog show one weekend, it all came to an end. We had stopped to exercise three of the pugs when a mongrel, its lips curled, approached. Aunt Beth hurried her two dogs back to the car, but I saw the cur as a challenge. I thought Mingo would feel the same way. So I slipped off his collar and commanded, "Sic 'im, Mingo!" Instead of charging, Mingo fled.

We spent the rest of that day searching and calling. When we had no luck, Aunt Beth hired other people to hunt for him. She offered a big reward for Mingo's return, but when no one succeeded, Aunt Beth gave up. She hasn't spoken to me since.

It's been like that all my life. Challenges I meet head-on have a way of boomeranging. The latest came about in Scouts when a new kid in town joined our troop. In the midst of first aid instruction, the scoutmaster was called to the telephone. Since I had earned a merit badge in first aid, I assumed he'd want me to take over. So I decided to demonstrate the fireman's carry. The new boy was big—a challenge—and I chose him as my "victim." When he backed away, trying to argue, I ducked under his arms and doubled him up over my left shoulder. He screamed and struggled.

By the time the scoutmaster came running it was too late. The boy had recently had an appendicitis operation and my "demonstration" had ripped open the incision. Everyone, of course, acted like I should be expelled from the troop. And the boy's parents threatened to sue the Scouts and my parents. That's when I was shipped off to Uncle Bob. He was a last resort.

Trying not to embarrass me, Uncle Bob acted as though there was no special reason for my visit. First he took me fishing. I knew it was just a stalling tactic. If we hadn't been interrupted by a deer crashing through the brush, a lecture most certainly would have followed. Instead, Uncle Bob only frowned and watched the deer leap over the stream and bound up the hill behind me. "They usually bed down this time of day," he said. "Something's panicked it . . . must be chasing it."

We stared up the hill across the stream. A weasel and a couple of rabbits came fleeing down. "It must be something big to make a weasel run," I said. "Maybe a bear."

"No bears around here," Uncle Bob muttered. "As I told you on the way out here, there hasn't been much wildlife in this area until recently because—"

The screaming clamor of blue jays, crows, and other birds drowned him out. But I knew what he'd been about to say.

Several years ago, after a nuclear explosion had started a radioactive cloud drifting across the Pacific, a heavy rain had brought most of the fallout down here, killing and misshaping wildlife and plants. No one had been allowed into this dangerous area for some time, but recent tests had shown the woods and hills to be safe. The area was once again opened for fishing, hiking, and camping.

"If it isn't a bear, then what . . . " I began, staring up toward a leafless tree killed by the fallout.

Uncle Bob reeled in his line. "What do you say we go back to the pickup." His voice had a false cheeriness about it and I wondered whether he was as scared as I was.

A heavy grunting made us jump. Looking up toward the rim of the hill, we both gasped. Looming into view, the sun behind it, a huge black silhouette stood snorting. Squinting into the sun made it hard for us to see details, but the huge black shape had a flat-topped head and large drooping ears that flapped in the breeze like an elephant's.

That was frightening enough. But when it turned its head to face us, its flattened nose and bulging, bowling-ball eyes made me feel weak in the knees. Each eye seemed to be surrounded by black fur, and a deep growl came from its tawny chest.

"Uncle Bob," I whispered. "What *is* it?"

"I don't know," he muttered. His voice shook. "Don't make any fast moves. Don't raise your voice. I don't think it's seen us yet. Let's move away . . . quietly . . . slowly . . . carefully. . . ."

Gingerly I started to reel in my line. The ratchety click sounded awfully loud. "Never mind that!" Uncle Bob snapped, keeping his voice down. "Just lay it down—leave it."

The sun must have glinted on my fishing rod, because the beast peered straight down at us. Growling deep in its throat, it stepped toward us. More of the immense body came into view. A tail, outlined in the gold of the sun, curled over its back. It waved menacingly from side to side.

As the beast stalked down into the shadows of the hill, we could see it in frightening detail. The fur was short for so huge a beast, and the face and ears were black. Dark furrows radiated from the broad brow to the top of the huge skull. I stood transfixed.

"Uncle Bob!"

He yanked my arm. "Come on. "

When we moved, the beast came faster. So did its growls. "It's too big—we'll never make it to the car," Uncle Bob cried.

"But Uncle Bob," I shouted. "Listen to me! I have an idea—"

I tripped over a boulder and went down. Uncle Bob hauled me to my feet. We raced ahead. I glanced back over my shoulder. The growling monster was gaining on us, crashing through the bushes as though they were mere weeds.

Uncle Bob pointed ahead toward a thick grove of lodgepole pines. "Get in there."

"But Uncle Bob!" The bounding beast was almost upon us.

"Keep going," he yelled, shoving me. He twisted around to face the charging beast. Waving his arms, he yelled. The beast knocked him tumbling, then swerved away beyond the bushes.

Uncle Bob didn't move. He just lay there, moaning. When I ran back I saw that his face was sweaty and sort of greenish white, and his leg, bent at an angle that shouldn't have been possible, looked even worse. His trouser leg was torn above the knee, and something jagged and white thrust through it. Blood stained the torn cloth. I knew from my first aid that this was a compound fracture.

"Uncle Bob," I gasped, not wanting to look. "There isn't time to splint. Can you try to hold on while I get you into the pines?"

He opened his pain-filled eyes and gestured with his head. "Never mind me. Get in there yourself. The trees are too close together for it to follow."

"That's okay," I said, and I tried to sit him up. Although he was heavy, I thought that if I could get him up into a fireman's carry we'd both make it.

"Get in there," he repeated as the growling grew louder.

I was so scared, the temptation to obey was almost overwhelming. But I couldn't leave Uncle Bob. I'd never be able to live with myself if I did.

Bushes crashed behind me and I spun around to face those monster eyes. Maybe it was bravery, or maybe I just reacted like a defiant mouse that squeaks when it's cornered. But for some reason, from deep inside me came a powerful yell. The beast braced to a stop. Yelling once more, I

grabbed a piece of broken limb and threw it. Surprisingly, the beast whirled back from sight into the bushes.

Jumping behind Uncle Bob, I got my hands in his armpits. Digging in my heels, I dragged him toward the lodgepole pines. He helped by shoving with his good leg. Once or twice he let go of his thigh to grasp trees to help me pull him to safety. At last we were deep into the grove of tall, close-growing trees. Outside, the mammoth animal sniffed and growled, stalking back and forth, looking for a way in after us.

Uncle Bob had fainted. His pants were soggy with blood, and when I tore his trouser leg open wider, the blood spurted. I knew then, from the first aid movie I'd seen in Scouts, that Uncle Bob needed a tourniquet.

Slipping off his belt, I looped it around his thigh close to the crotch, placed a wadded handkerchief over where the severed artery should be, then used a stick to twist and tighten the belt. When I finished, Uncle Bob regained consciousness.

"Thanks," he murmured. When I asked if he could hold the tourniquet, he nodded.

By the time I had gathered pine needles to make a softer bed for him, it was almost dark. I crept toward the edge of the grove. The beast was waiting. Though it was lying down with its head resting on gigantic clawed feet, its eyes were wide open and alert. It must have spotted me because immediately it jerked its head in my direction. Bouncing to its feet, it growled, and I fled back to Uncle Bob.

He'd fainted again. His hand had slipped from the tourniquet, and though I knew it should be loosened every so often, I wondered how much blood Uncle Bob had lost and how much more he could afford to lose.

Tightening the belt, I caught an end of the stick in one of his belt loops. Now I could safely let go of it. But what could I do instead? Sitting there in the darkness, shivering in the night chill, I really didn't know.

Uncle Bob needed a doctor, a hospital. Help would be needed to move him. If I could get to the pickup, parked about a half mile away, I could call for help on the CB, the citizens' band two-way radio.

The pitch-black night had substance. It shook with the growls and snorts of the beast as I eased toward the far side of the lodgepole pines. At the edge of the grove I peered out into the open darkness. The sounds of the beast were far behind me. All I had to do now was move toward the pickup as quietly as possible.

But I couldn't do it. I'd forgotten to get the keys. I'd need them to unlock the pickup and the ignition lock. Otherwise the CB wouldn't work.

Ashamed as I am now to admit it, I was *glad* I didn't have to leave the shelter of the pines. And when the beast suddenly came raging and snorting around the grove I felt relieved and lucky as well.

Scrambling back into the pines, I tried to move silently. But the darkness became thicker, and behind me, the creature tried to thrust into the pines. Limbs swayed overhead. The big nostrils snorted in frustration. A blast of its hot breath swept pine needles up and around me.

Crawling around in my fright, I lost my way. I couldn't find Uncle Bob. Bumping into trees, I called softly but there was no answer, and thoughts of how I never should have left him alone plagued me. Suppose the tourniquet had loosened. Suppose he was bleeding to death. It would be my fault. Once again I'd tried to tackle something too big for me. I shivered because I was cold and because I was scared. Maybe I was crying a little, too.

Then I heard a sort of sobbing sound—this time not my own. Pausing, I listened until it came again. It was a moaning sob and I crawled toward it. Finally, I found

Uncle Bob. He was delirious.

Carefully loosening the tourniquet, I detected no sign of new bleeding, and throughout the rest of that horrible night—listening to his moans—I checked it from time to time. It would have been easier if I could have talked to him—gotten his advice—but it was just me and that rumbling monster. Uncle Bob stayed unconscious, and I was going to have to face things—the beast and myself—alone.

Along toward dawn, when my eyes had adjusted to the darkness, I got Uncle Bob's car keys. Then, shivering, I removed my shirt and tore it into strips to bandage his thigh. With more strips of shirt and two strong lengths of fallen branches, I splinted his broken thigh the way I'd been taught in Scouts. I'd never splinted a real fracture before, and I hoped it was all right.

The grayness of dawn had begun to sneak through the trees by the time I had finished. So I crept toward the edge of the pines where the rhythmic sounds of the beast were louder. Peering out at the huge, lion-colored form, I saw that its eyes were closed. It was asleep. Those rumbling sounds that had terrified me throughout the night were *snores!*

Moving quietly to the far side of the grove I paused, breathing hard, shivering and sweating. Maybe I should just stay with Uncle Bob until people came looking for us. I'd be alive, but would Uncle Bob?

Breathing deeply, I stepped out from the lodgepole pines. My legs felt like wood, and fright was like a beast inside me, trying to get out. I had to force myself not to look back. I had to keep going. If it rushed after me, I'd certainly hear it.

The pickup was on the other side of a little hill just ahead of me. I wanted to run but knew that the noise would wake the beast. When I finally reached the brow of the hill, a band of sunlight added a rosy tinge to the clouds and

98

glinted off the windshield. It was an encouraging sight and I moved ahead too eagerly. A rock tumbled down the hill.

Back by the pines a faint snore became a startled eruption of sound. Though I couldn't yet see the beast, the blasts of barking sounds were enough to convince me to run. Scrambling down the hill, practically falling, I glanced over my shoulder. It was going to be close. Frantically I dug into my pockets for the keys. Maybe I wouldn't make it.

Both my mind and body raced. I thought of my conversation with Uncle Bob yesterday and about all the things I wanted to tell him during the night. Now, with no assurance that I might be right, I was going to have to face it alone. The clicking of the beast's huge claws on the rocks behind me was a terrifying reminder.

Fumbling with the keys, turning them in the lock, I felt the creature's hot breath. The door was open! But the beast was there, blocking me from shutting it. I scurried back across the seat. It was the moment of truth.

Uncle Bob kept a revolver in the glove compartment. He had taught me how to use it, but I hesitated. A revolver bullet? Big-game hunters used special high-powered rifles. A revolver bullet would only make the beast angry. It would never kill it.

The beast rocked the pickup in its efforts to get to me. Any moment it was apt to turn the whole thing over and wreck the CB radio antenna. And then what? I reached toward the glove compartment. Maybe I should take a chance and try shooting at it. Or maybe I should take a different chance—one I had wanted to discuss with Uncle Bob.

I had my hand on the glove compartment but I didn't open it. I faced the huge pug-nosed face that was slobbering and growling through the open door. In that instant, fragments of my first impressions of the beast began to fit together. Or did they? Maybe it was just wishful thinking. Maybe I'd better get the gun.

The monster growled deep in its throat, its hot breath steaming the windshield. The pickup rocked wildly. I braced against the dash and clung to the steering wheel. I shouted, but this time it was not a meaningless, frightened yell. The fright was there, of course, but this time I shouted words—commands. And if I were wrong—if they had no effect?

"No! Down! Stay!" Somehow my aching lungs took in another breath. "Down! Stay, Mingo, stay! Mingo . . ."

Yes, the beast *did* look like a mammoth Chinese pug. It had the same coloring, face, and grunting sounds of Aunt Beth's Mingo. That's what I had wanted to discuss with Uncle Bob last night. I wanted to know if he thought it possible that the radioactive rain could have caused a dog to grow to such an unbelievable size. Mingo had been lost just before that destructive drenching rain, and this giant creature, despite its size, strongly resembled that tiny champion pug.

"Mingo!" I shouted again. "Down! Sit!"

Did those eyes look less angry? Were they ever really angry or were they just alight with the friendliness of a lonely pet? I yelled to make myself heard above the loud, puglike grunting sounds. "Mingo! Sit! Sit, Mingo!"

For a horrible moment he stared, blowing his breath into my face. Then he backed off and sat on the ground, his head as high as the cab roof, his eyes alert, his breath quick and eager.

"Good boy," I said, my voice shaking and squeaking. "Good boy. Stay, Mingo."

I put the key in the ignition switch, turned it, then called into the CB mike. "Ten thirty-three. Ten thirty-three." That was the emergency CB distress call. Voices answered. I told the CBers—and the police who had also tuned in—what had happened and where to find us. Before I signed off I had one more urgent thing to say.

"Please, do not be frightened by the big animal with me. He's just an oversized friendly dog. Please do not think you have to shoot him. *Please!*"

Later that day when I was finally able to visit Uncle Bob in the hospital, I told him how I had helped get Mingo to a high-fenced corral belonging to a veterinarian who specialized in treating large animals. Everyone—the vet, doctors, and scientists—all thanked me for alerting the police not to kill Mingo, large and fearsome as he looked. He was going to be a great source of study and research, and privately, for Aunt Beth's sake, I hoped they might even discover how to get him back to normal size.

When I finished my story, Uncle Bob gave me a funny little smile. "I think the biggest discovery has already been made," he said. "And you made it when you faced up to something big without a chip on your shoulder."

I nodded, beginning to understand. "If I'd grabbed your gun, I could have spoiled it all by shooting at Mingo. And," I admitted sheepishly, "I guess I've spoiled a lot of things because . . . because they were bigger than me . . . and because I was just a runt. . . ."

Uncle Bob smiled. "What matters is how big you are inside." He reached out and grasped my hand. "Thanks for what you did for me."

It was great to shake his hand and not have him mad at me for something I'd done wrong. It was a nice feeling and I was going to try and keep it that way—from now on.

you Are what you Eat

by WILMA BEDNARZ

Kevin Wheatmore thought how unfair it was to be twelve and have to trim the hedge instead of reading his new book on interplanetary survival.

"Didn't you know two weeks ago about the book report?" his father asked.

"Sure, but you don't understand. . . ." He didn't say any more. He never knew how to answer questions like that.

"Be as sullen as you want, but finish that hedge." His father returned to the other side of the house and Kevin heard him start the lawn mower. Then, over the mower's drone, he heard a jetlike whine that came closer and closer.

A fireball circled the house next door, smashing into the chimney. A loud explosion resulted and the house went up in flames.

Just before it struck the chimney, a green opalescent figure emerged from the burning machine. It darted convulsively back and forth over the houses before diving into the Holmans' back yard.

"Call the fire department, Mom," Kevin shouted as his mother ran out on the front porch. "I'll see if they need help getting out of the house." He ran toward the rear. The Holmans' back door was usually open.

Fourteen-year-old Joyce Holman was a good friend. Kevin had seen her return home on her bike about half an hour ago, and when he reached their yard, he was relieved to see that both Joyce and her parents were safe. They were gathered around the green creature that had flattened their zinnia bed.

The thing was as large as the outdoor cooker nearby, and it was shaped like the wasp pupae he and Joyce had found last summer. But this thing was not dormant. Pulsing and wiggling, its wing pads, feelers, mouth parts, and legs were tightly folded against its body. It smelled like fermenting grass.

As Kevin hurried toward the group, he saw a green appendage whip toward Mr. Holman. Another wrapped around Joyce and her mother. A green quivering mass enveloped them. Mr. Holman's hammer dropped to the ground. The Holmans were gone.

Kevin's stomach surged but he grabbed a board leaning against the fence and ran toward the monster.

"You can't get away with that. Joyce is my friend. The Holmans are our neighbors."

He struck the monster with the board only to have it jerked away from him.

As he watched the contorting insect body, Kevin thought he was going crazy. Moving like dough being kneaded, it took on the form of Joyce Holman. It reached toward Kevin.

"Don't you touch me," he shouted. But before he could dodge the green hand, it grabbed his wrist. A painful burning sensation spread across his skin. His arm was being drawn into the monster. He screamed.

For a moment Kevin thought it was his scream that made the monster drop his arm, but it must have been the fire sirens as the engines blasted their arrival. The creature clapped its hands over its ears—Joyce's ears.

"I forgot about the cursed sounds of this planet," a voice that sounded like Joyce's said. The thing had taken on the insect shape again, but as the sirens began to wind down, Joyce's figure returned. This time a flesh color spread over the skin, and short brown hair curled over the head. Except for the bloodshot eyes that glared at Kevin from an angry face, it looked just like Joyce.

Firemen, dragging extension ladders, hoses, and chemical packs, came around the house. Kevin's mother and dad were with them. Mrs. Wheatmore rushed toward Joyce.

"Don't touch her, Mom. She's a monster!"

"Oh, Kevin!" Mrs. Wheatmore took Joyce in her arms and nothing happened.

"My mother and dad! They're in there!" Joyce pointed to the burning house. Firemen were just about to dart into it when the roof collapsed. Kevin's mother and father tried to console Joyce.

"Mom! Dad! Be careful! She ate the Holmans!" Kevin shouted. "That's not Joyce, I tell you. She's a monster!"

"Kevin, that's enough," roared his father.

"Excuse me, mister, but the kid is suffering from shock," one of the firemen said. "Nothing could live in that building. He knows it. Look at the burn on his arm. He's a brave kid. Must have tried to save them."

The Wheatmores took Kevin and Joyce home, and Dr. Brennan was called to treat Kevin's arm.

"This shot will put you to sleep for a while," Dr. Brennan said. "When you wake up, everything will be all right."

"No, you've got to listen to me. . . ." The injection took effect.

It was late in the evening when Kevin woke up. The pain in his bandaged arm brought back the memory of the fire and the Holmans. He sat upright in bed. Were his mother and dad safe? Where was the space alien now?

Suddenly he was aware that his door was opening, and that a strong odor of fermenting grass permeated the room. The creature, using only the rough figure of a human body to allow it to walk, stood in the doorway. "I want you," it said. "I need your help." Its voice began with Mr. Holman's deep tone and pitched to Joyce's voice.

"What have you done with my mother and dad?" Kevin didn't know that anyone whose heart was pounding as hard as his could still live.

"Your mother and father are downstairs watching television—the noise box. I need them so that everything will seem normal until the pack arrives on this planet."

"What planet do you come from?"

"From Olgorin. In two weeks Olgorin will be in a positive position to condense messages from earth via the nuclear frequency accelerator. Then my pack will swarm. But you must help me find a quiet place where I can send my signals. There are too many city sounds here."

"This pack—are they like you?"

"Of course. We are creatwasps. I'm in a stage of travel transformation and I need food."

"Is everyone on Olgorin like you?"

"We are the only ones remaining now. That is why I am here as a scout."

"What you mean is that you're coming here for food. *We* would be your food." Kevin found it difficult not to scream at the creature. "There are small animals in the fields along the highways on the edge of town. Why don't you eat them?" The creatwasp didn't answer. It only shrugged its half-human shoulders and left the room.

It was decided that because Joyce's only relative was a

bachelor uncle who traveled, Joyce would stay with the Wheatmores. She settled into the guest room.

The creatwasp had been able to take over Joyce's figure, voice, and mannerisms so well that it had no identity trouble with her friends or teachers. Only Kevin could not forget what she was, and the urgency of proving this to others before the creatwasp pack swarmed to earth got him into trouble. He tried again to warn his father, but it accomplished nothing.

"Tell me, Kevin. Hasn't Joyce always been your friend? Didn't she teach you to dive rather than belly flop last summer?"

"But that was Joyce, Dad. This is a creatwasp. You read about all the cats and dogs that are missing. Well, Joyce—"

"Stop it. That's a terrible thing to say about the poor girl."

"Dad, just smell her. You'll know."

"That's enough, Kevin." The subject was closed.

A week after the fire, Kevin took the homeroom attendance record to the office where the principal's door was open. Joyce was in the room with him, and Kevin could hear some of their conversation.

"I know that you have gone through a terrible experience, Joyce, but it doesn't give you the right to be impertinent. Miss Jones told me that when she asked you to put the algebra problem on the board, you barked at her."

"Meow, meow," Joyce answered. From where he stood, Kevin saw the back of Joyce's neck turn green. She was having trouble controlling herself. When Joyce noticed him, Kevin hurried out of the office.

Two days later the newspaper carried the story of the principal's disappearance. "No clues ... no notes ... no ransom letters," Mr. Wheatmore sighed, quoting the newspaper at dinner.

"Kevin, eat your dinner," his mother said. "You're getting so thin."

"I'm really not hungry. I've got so much homework, I'd like to be excused."

Waiting upstairs until he heard Joyce go to her room, Kevin turned on his favorite radio station. It was rock—the Mama Bugs. He liked to listen at full volume. Soon his parents would settle down in front of the television and he could talk to Joyce. He didn't really expect her to listen to reason though.

"Come in." The creatwasp's voice sounded like the school principal's. Opening the door, Kevin was repulsed at what he saw. Though the creatwasp was partially in its original shape, its head was a green version of Joyce's, collie paws rested on the arms of the chair, and a cat's tail twitched from the insect body.

"Turn off that radio!" The creatwasp lunged at him, placing two collie paws on his chest. Kevin shoved against it with both hands.

"Do it now!" Strong insect mandibles thrust near his face.

"Let me go and I'll turn it off."

The creatwasp followed Kevin across the hall to his room. As he snapped off the radio, the creatwasp returned to Joyce's form, though it still had some difficulty with the collie paws.

"Small animals do not agree with me," the creatwasp said. "You saw what happened in the principal's office the other day."

The fermenting grass odor was heavy in the room. Something—possibly the smaller animals that did not agree with it—had weakened the creature. This could be his chance to get rid of it!

Kevin waited until the house was dark and quiet. Taking the only weapon he could find, a baseball bat, he went into the hall. When his bare feet made a brushing sound on the carpet, he stopped. But the house remained still.

The guest room door made only the softest click as Kevin pushed it. The drapes were open, and the moonlight showed the creatwasp in a resting position on the bed, its green feelers extended two feet in front of it. The creatwasp sprang up.

"Help! Help! He's going to hit me! Help!" Joyce's voice rang through the house. Lights flashed on in the hall.

"What's going on here?" Kevin's father grabbed the baseball bat.

"He's crazy!" the creatwasp sobbed, looking exactly like Joyce, and Mrs. Wheatmore put her arms around her.

"Into your room, young man," his father said.

"But Dad—"

"We'll talk about it in the morning." When his father left, he locked the door to Kevin's room from the outside.

It was late the next morning when Kevin's mother called him for breakfast. "I'm late for school," he shouted.

"You're not going to school today. I made an appointment with the doctor for you this morning."

"I suppose you mean a psychiatrist. There's nothing wrong with me, if you would only listen."

"Shhh, don't get excited."

The psychiatrist reminded the Wheatmores that the experience of the fire and the deaths of the Holmans had been more than Kevin had been able to accept.

"It will take time," he said. "Didn't you mention that his grandfather lives on a farm? Perhaps a change would help. Why don't you send him there?"

Kevin boarded the jet that afternoon. Though the trip took only two hours, and the stewardess in charge of him was kind, it seemed longer. His grandfather was waiting at the airport.

Kevin had never been able to talk to his grandfather, whose favorite question was, "How's school?" How do you answer a question like that? He would never be able to convince him that there was such a thing as a creatwasp and that its message must be stopped.

It was about twenty-five miles from the airport to the farm. As they drove, his grandfather did most of the talking. "You can ride that colt now that you admired so much last summer." Kevin thanked him and a long silence followed.

"How's school?" his grandfather asked, nervously clearing his throat.

"Great. I got the second highest math grade." Kevin went on to tell him about the magazine rack he was building in shop because it seemed now that it was his grandfather who needed to be put at ease. He asked such questions only because he didn't know what else to say.

By the middle of the week Kevin felt at home on the farm. If it were not for the realization that the creatwasp's message would go to Olgorin on Saturday and that by Sunday they'd all be gone, Kevin would have been happy.

Kevin was grooming the colt in its stall while his grandfather mended a feeder at the other end of the barn. The farmyard was noisy. Chickens, dogs, and horses made most of the sounds, and Kevin had an idea.

"Grandpa, I've got to talk to you. You've got to listen to me."

"Try me," his grandfather said.

So Kevin told him all about the creatwasp and its plans for Saturday. Grandfather wrinkled his forehead. "What you're saying is serious, Kevin. Can you prove any of it?"

"Look at this!" Kevin desperately tore the bandage from his wrist. "See the claw prints? I wasn't burned in the fire."

109   Grandfather Wheatmore gave a low whistle. "Your

story sounds incredible, Kevin, but I believe you. Do you have any idea how we can get rid of this thing?"

"I do now," Kevin said. "I know that it's not what it eats that weakens it, as I first thought. . . ." And he went on to describe his plan.

"There's one thing wrong," his grandfather said. "Your parents won't let Joyce come up here. Only a few days ago you attacked her with a baseball bat!"

"But, don't you see, Grandpa. Joyce is the creatwasp, and if you mention how quiet it is up here, she'll come anyway. She needs the silence."

The trap was set the way Kevin suggested, and Kevin tested it several times to make sure it worked. Early the following Saturday, Joyce arrived. Kevin knew that if his trap didn't work by afternoon, he and everyone else would be dead. But as they talked, the creature looked so much like Joyce, with the same voice and mannerisms, that Kevin began to wonder if maybe his parents and the psychiatrist were right. His grandfather looked doubtful, too.

"I'd like to see the farm," Joyce said after a short time, and Kevin, anxious to try his plan before his grandfather changed his mind, went into his act.

"There's nothing special about it," Kevin said, pretending he didn't want to show her around.

"Where is the quiet place?" Joyce asked, grimacing at the clucking chickens.

"I'll show you later. Come on, you'll like the barn."

"What's in the barn?" Joyce stopped to look at a kitten playing with a piece of string.

"The horses. I'll show you the horses." Kevin hadn't intended for his voice to sound so eager.

"No, thanks. I've tried them. I mean, I know what a horse looks like."

"There's a calf."

"A what? Oh, I want to see it," Joyce said, and she

110

followed him toward the barn. Just at the door, though, she clapped her hands over her ears.

"Kevin, I can't stand those squawking chickens. I've got to get away from here." Green splotches spread across Joyce's forehead.

"No, you've got to see the calf," he yelled, and careful only to touch her coat, he shoved her through the barn door. At the same time he kicked the hidden switch he had set up under the straw.

Bells rang. Radios tuned to different stations and set at full volume blared. Records of train whistles, fire sirens, and factory whistles played on old phonographs. Kevin and his grandfather had even dragged in an old dinner bell that was used to warn the neighbors in case of fire. Operating electrically, it clanged loudly.

All this came over the amplifier at multiple volume. The horses, frightened at the noise, began to neigh. Kevin blew on his athletic whistle and directed the piercing sound right into Joyce's ear.

The plan was working. Joyce began to turn green. Her features blurred, forming the insect eyes and heavy mandibles of the creatwasp. Long wasplike legs appeared, and her body slimmed out to a hornet shape. The odor of fermenting grass dominated the smell of the hay and the horses.

Grandpa Wheatmore, who had followed them to the barn, watched what used to be Joyce. "Look out, Kevin," he cried. "The dinner bell has stopped. The creature will get back its strength."

Kevin saw that the bell mechanism had broken down. The creatwasp was stretching up on its legs, reaching toward Grandpa Wheatmore. Kevin grabbed the bell's rope and yanked, ringing it over and over until the creatwasp collapsed.

Kevin did not stop ringing the bell or blowing his whistle until the monster, now nothing but a green quiver-

ing mass, shriveled and was still.

They put it into a box and nailed it shut. "The UFO Investigation Committee will want to see this," Grandfather Wheatmore said.

The following Wednesday, in the living room of his own home, Kevin held out his hand to receive the engraved commendation from General Greene. His mother, father, and grandfather watched proudly.

". . . for your brave contribution to both science and your country," General Greene was saying. "Through you a grave danger to the people of this planet has been removed."

A photographer's flash unit went off and the ceremony ended.

"You saw your duty and you did it." Mr. Wheatmore patted Kevin's shoulder. "But there's more to be done. Look how the hedge has grown. You'll find the clippers in the garage."

Nightmare in a Box

by RITA RITCHIE

Tracy Ann Stuart huddled in the far corner of the dark fruit cellar, her heart thumping as she listened to the creature prowling outside the door.

She could hear its harsh breathing and the scraping of its nails on the wooden panels. Had it found her at last?

Abruptly the pawing stopped. There was an irritable, questing rumble deep in the monster's throat. Then the swish-thump of its movement began to recede.

Tracy crept to the door and peered through the latch hole. She could see the creature in the occasional shafts of evening sun shining through the tiny basement windows. The hideous thing was big now, bigger than her father, and it was methodically scrabbling in the various corners of the old basement. It would move fast enough, she knew, once it found its prey.

The quill-like growths on the monster's back were now long fleshy tubes, and the flexible nose of the misshapen purple face extended like a baby elephant's. The yellow horns looked harder and sharper, while the red eyes . . . You did not need much light to see those malevolent red eyes.

Tracy wished again with all her might that she had never taken that package inside the house. When the doorbell rang that afternoon, Tracy had been alone most of the day in the big old house that was the Stuart family's new home.

At twelve, Tracy was old enough to be left in charge while her parents made one last trip to their former home over a hundred miles away for the final load of personal belongings. Someone had to stay here to admit the telephone people, in case this was the day they chose to install the phone. Her parents had hardly left after breakfast when a lady came to read the water meter. Staying a little while to chat, she told Tracy something of the neighborhood. Now at last the telephone people had arrived.

But it was not a telephone company truck Tracy saw when she pulled open the heavy front door. Instead, a large red van was parked in the gravel driveway, and a man in a brown uniform stood on the steps holding a box. The man said, "National Package Delivery. Can I leave this shipment with you? The lady down the road isn't home."

Tracy hesitated, then remembered her mother taking in things for their neighbors in their old town. She nodded. "Okay. How do I know where to take it?"

The man set the package down and scribbled in his notebook. "You don't have to do anything, miss. I'll just leave a notice in her door and she can come for it when she gets home." He thrust pencil and pad at Tracy. "Sign here, please."

She wrote her name carefully. "Who is the package for?"

"Name's Cranshaw. Lives in that green house down there. Thanks, miss!" He walked vigorously to his van, hopped in, and drove off, leaving Tracy with her mouth open in dismay.

"Cranshaw!" she repeated, looking down the road at

the home of their nearest neighbor. Here at the edge of town, the houses became widely scattered and were not at all like those in the suburb where Tracy had spent most of her life. And the ramshackle dark green house down the road, half-hidden behind a luxurious growth of spooky-looking pine trees, seemed like the kind of house a witch would live in. "Creepy" Cranshaw they called her in town, or so said the water meter lady. Tracy shivered, then remembered the package.

The box was perfectly ordinary looking, wrapped in brown paper and sturdily tied with cord. It had a neat white label bearing the name of Miss Lulu Cranshaw, but no return address. Big red stickers with white letters fairly shouted FRAGILE! DO NOT DROP! KEEP OUT OF LIGHT! And here the midafternoon sun was pouring its warm rays down upon it.

Tracy was reluctant to touch anything destined for a witch. But she did not want Miss Cranshaw angry with her, either. So she picked it up carefully, surprised at its light weight, and set it down in a dark corner of the entry. Now it was just an ordinary package waiting for its owner to claim it.

While she washed the set of good dishes her mother had unpacked that morning, Tracy began to wonder what a witch would order through the mail. Maybe it was a surprise sent by somebody else—a relative, or another witch.

The wondering about the box became an itch in Tracy's mind. Drying the last of the dishes and putting them in the cupboard, she went to look at the box sitting in the shadowed entry.

She flipped on the light switch. A *little* light could not hurt. Then she gently raised the box a few inches off the floor and shook it. There was a faint rustling, like crunched-up newspaper. Maybe somebody sent the box for a joke. Or maybe—Tracy's throat got tight—maybe it was a doll to stick pins in!

The flaps of the neatly folded wrapping paper were not stuck down with tape. And the stiff cord was loose enough to slip off, if somebody wanted to.

Tracy slipped it off. She unfolded the brown paper to reveal a gray cardboard box. She lifted off the lid.

Tucked in a nest of crushed newspaper was something wrapped in black paper. It was irregular in shape, with the paper twisted around so that nobody would ever notice a couple of extra creases. Standing up under the entry light, Tracy untwisted the paper and opened it.

For a second or two she stared at the horrible little dried-up thing in her hand. Then shuddering with revulsion, she flung it away and ran back to the kitchen. There she soaped her hands under the running faucet, washing and scrubbing, trying to forget the dreadful image.

It had been alive once, but Tracy had never even imagined an animal like that, not in her most awful nightmares. She remembered a stupid joke from way back in fourth grade. What does a witch ride on? A night mare. Ha-ha-ha.

But nobody would laugh at this nightmare. The dessicated body was purple-gray, with stickerlike things like porcupine quills over part of it. The underside was covered with mangy gray fur, half-hidden under the folded dead paws that looked like tiny clenched fists. But the face! It was a parody of a human face, with purple bulbous features, cracked and wrinkled, and with a tiny pair of yellow horns on the forehead. The nearly closed red eyes seemed to stare.

Ugh! Tracy shivered as she wiped her hands on a towel. Then she hugged herself, standing alone and nervous in the brightly painted kitchen. Her parents would not be home for at least a couple more hours, maybe even longer. Meanwhile, if Miss Lulu Cranshaw came and asked for her package . . . She would be awfully angry that it had been opened.

Remembering the stories the water meter lady had told her about "Creepy" Cranshaw, Tracy knew she had to put the package back together. She rehearsed it in her mind. She would just march in, quickly wrap up the little dead monster, and jam it back in the box. Taking a determined breath, she walked swiftly to the front entry. Trying not to think about it, she scooped up the black paper.

It was empty.

The dreadful little dried-up thing must have fallen out when she had thrown it. Tracy looked around carefully, then stooped to feel the patterned rug with her hands. Sick at the thought of touching the thing, she knew she had to.

Except for the box and its wrappings, the entry was completely bare. Tracy shook out the paper, cord, and box, but found nothing. She wondered how she could fail to see the little monster under the entry light.

Light. *Keep Out of Light!*

Maybe light had somehow made it disappear. It was a crazy idea—about as crazy as having a witch living just down the road. But Tracy snapped off the light anyway.

Going into the living room, she glanced around, hoping the nasty little husk had rolled in there. Light flooded in through the windows, but the wide expanse of carpet was bare. The furniture was too far away for it to have—

What was that?

A quick movement flickered at the edge of her vision, but when Tracy turned her head she saw nothing out of the ordinary. Maybe it was just a bird shadow flashing across the window. She glanced outside.

A face stared back at her. It was an old woman's face, pointed and wrinkled, and piercing dark eyes locked into Tracy's. The woman on the porch stepped closer and held up the National Package Delivery slip in a bony hand.

Swallowing hard, Tracy numbly went to open the front door.

"I'm Miss Lulu Cranshaw," said a voice as spiky as a

dried milkweed pod. As the breeze pulled her dress against her, her tall spindly frame was revealed. An old-fashioned car was parked in front of the house. "You have a package for me."

Tracy's breath hurt as she said, "No, ma'am, we haven't got a package or anything."

Miss Cranshaw pursed her lips. She held out the delivery notice. "This *is* 26445 Baxter, isn't it?"

"Yes, it is. I was home all day and nobody came." She waited a moment and when Miss Cranshaw did not move, Tracy added, "I guess somebody made a mistake."

"I am your nearest neighbor, Miss Tracy Ann Stuart. I think we should start out being friendly."

It sounded like a threat. Tracy's momentary wavering hardened into a resolve to carry the charade through. "Yes, Miss Cranshaw. I'll look around to see if I can find anything. And I'll ask my parents when they come home."

"This package," said Miss Cranshaw, speaking slowly and distinctly, "has a very special pet inside. It needs a certain kind of care. If it is not treated correctly, it can be *fatal*."

"I'll look for the box," Tracy said, thinking desperately, *Go away, please!*

"I will go now," said Miss Cranshaw, grinning a knowing grin. "When you find my little pet, come and tell me immediately. You don't have much time—perhaps an hour, maybe less. Then it will be too late." She turned on her heel and went to her car.

Relieved, Tracy shut the door and locked it. But as she turned, her eye caught the jumble of box and wrappings lying exactly where light from the opened door would fall upon it.

Had Miss Cranshaw seen it?

If so, she knew now that Tracy had opened her box. Maybe that's why she had given her a time limit to restore the contents—or suffer dreadful witch consequences!

Tracy had to find that horrible thing, box it up, then tell Miss Cranshaw she found it near the back door. She would search hard all over for it, now, before her parents came home.

Once more a shadow fluttered in a corner of the living room, a larger one this time. Maybe a cat had gotten into the house. And if it found that dried-up "pet" and tore it to pieces . . .

Tracy had plenty of experience with other people's cats. "Here, kitty!" She pulled out the easy chair.

Gazing into evil red eyes, Tracy froze. The creature was no longer a dehydrated husk. It was fleshed out to five times the original size. The fists clasped and unclasped, the dreadful bulbous nose wriggled, and down in its throat was a rattle and a hiss.

It was alive!

Tracy screamed. She tore into the kitchen, slamming the door behind her.

When she stopped shaking, she forced herself to think. She did not understand about the witch's pet coming alive, but she knew she had to deal with it. If she could just think of that wretched monster as a dreadful kind of cat, she could manage it.

Armed with a broom and the strongest carton she could find, Tracy quietly sidled out of the kitchen, sneaked down the long dark hall past the basement door, and slipped into the living room.

Grimly she advanced on the easy chair corner, but she found it empty. Wedging the box at one end of the space behind the nearby sofa, Tracy shoved the broom down along the wall toward it. She met with nothing.

Something snuffled behind her.

The creature, a yard tall, was standing on hind legs in the doorway to the dining room.

120   Tracy felt her insides dissolve into ice water.

The monster took a step toward her, hissing.

Tracy panicked. Stifling her sobs, she sped upstairs to her room, locked herself in, and cowered behind the door.

The hideous thing was *growing*! Something—maybe light—had started it, and now it was getting bigger.

She went to her window and looked down to the concrete walk two stories below. There was no way down, nothing to climb on. She could not jump without risking broken bones. The only way out of the house was to go downstairs. She would try to leave through the kitchen.

Tracy listened a long while, but if the monster were prowling downstairs, she could not hear it.

One fast dash—

Tracy reached the downstairs hall at running speed. At the bottom she leaped toward the kitchen.

Suddenly the creature reared up in front of her, tall and dreadful, arms poised as if to catch her. Shocked, Tracy sagged against the basement door. Then quickly she jerked it open and all but fell down the steps.

She blundered into shadowed dead ends and sections of wall, for this old basement was divided into many odd rooms. At last, in a far corner, she thrust open a door, stumbled through, and slammed it behind her. Her fingers encountered a snap lock, and she clicked it shut.

Tracy blinked in the gloom, for the dusty window set high in the wall was on the shady side of the house. She made out some old mason jars on gritty shelves. One of the long boards was loose, and she managed to wedge it behind some big bent nails on either side of the door, barring it against the monster, whose strength must be growing as its size increased.

It was not long before Tracy heard the creature moving around in the basement. The monster snuffled through the different sections, came to the fruit cellar door and scratched, then went away to search elsewhere.

The sun had nearly set. Surely her parents would soon come home! Then she remembered that as they left that morning her mother had said, "Since this is our last trip back and we have so much to do, Tracy, you're not to worry if we don't return before night." Not to worry! All Tracy had done was let loose a horror in their home.

A strong weight thudded against the door, and the crack of splintering wood was like a knife of fear through her heart. Somehow, by sound or smell or increased sharpening of its growing senses, the monster had found her!

Tracy scrambled up the shelves under the window, but the frame was nailed shut. Then her fingers gripped a piece of old pipe. Though she smashed the glass, the sound was lost under the crashing of the door. Pounding out the jagged

edges, Tracy squeezed through, sobbing as the glass scratched through her clothing. But she was free!

She hurtled through the dark underbrush separating the house from the Cranshaw place, and she warded off small branches that raked her as she plunged past. Then she fell with a painful thump into a dark hollow.

Tracy lay, waiting for her breath to come back. Bushes crackled above the hollow, and she heard the unmistakable snuffling of the dreadful beast. She closed her eyes, frozen with fear, waiting.

The crackling and the snuffling slowly went away.

Tracy squeezed her eyes tighter and concentrated on listening. At last she was convinced that the monster was really gone.

Tracy crawled up to the lip of the hollow. Not far from her a light from the Cranshaw place shone down a smooth woods path. Tracy sprang up and ran down the path, throwing herself at the door. Pounding on it, she cried, "Miss Cranshaw! Let me in!"

The door opened and she fell into Miss Cranshaw's arms. Tracy sobbed out her confession. "I opened the box, Miss Cranshaw, and the thing inside, the monster—"

"Hush, child! Come in." The old lady, surprisingly strong, pulled Tracy inside and turned the key. "So, you let loose something you did not know how to control."

"It's after me, Miss Cranshaw," Tracy babbled. "You can stop it. You're a witch. Save me!"

Miss Cranshaw grinned her dreadful knowing grin, and shook her head. "It's too late, Miss Tracy Ann Stuart. An hour after light falls upon it—"

"It's not too late, Miss Cranshaw!" Tracy's arm hurt where the old lady clutched it. "The monster's alive. It's growing bigger all the time!"

"That's right," Miss Cranshaw said firmly, pulling Tracy to a door in the wall. "While small, it did not matter. But now it's too late, my dear, because it is a full-sized monster—and you *know*." She thrust Tracy into a dimly lighted room and locked the door.

Tracy hammered on the door. "Miss Cranshaw, don't lock me up! I didn't mean—"

A dreadful snuffling stopped her in midsentence.

She turned, and there it was, the nightmare from the box, hideous head nearly touching the ceiling. The evil red eyes gleamed and a harsh voice came from the dreadful mouth. "Hello, Tracy," the monster said, reaching out for her.

124

PRINTED IN U.S.A.